His heart pounded with worry about what could be wrong.

A knock sounded at the door. Then another and another.

"William?" Julianne's plaintive voice.

He threw open the door. "Are you all right?"

She stood on his doorstep, her hair wet, her eyes wide and confusion in her gaze.

"What's wrong?" he asked.

"The man in the bandanna came back," Julianne said. "He hovered around outside and then disappeared. I was wrong about remaining at my house. I can't stay there alone, William."

He opened his arms and pulled her inside, feeling the beating of her heart and the softness of her embrace.

"Who's doing this, William?" Julianne dropped her head in her hands. "Someone wants me to leave my property. I don't know why, but I need to find out who it is and why he wants to do me harm. I..."

She looked up at him. Her eyes glistened with tears. "I need your help. I can't do it alone."

Debby Giusti is an award-winning Christian author who met and married her military husband at Fort Knox, Kentucky. Together they traveled the world, raised three wonderful children and have now settled in Atlanta, Georgia, where Debby spins tales of mystery and suspense that touch the heart and soul. Visit Debby online at debbygiusti.com, blog with her at seekerville.blogspot.com and craftieladiesofromance.blogspot.com, and email her at Debby@DebbyGiusti.com.

Books by Debby Giusti

Love Inspired Suspense

Her Forgotten Amish Past
Dangerous Amish Inheritance
Amish Christmas Search
Hidden Amish Secrets

Amish Witness Protection

Amish Safe House

Amish Protectors

Amish Refuge
Undercover Amish
Amish Rescue
Amish Christmas Secrets

Visit the Author Profile page at Harlequin.com for more titles.

HIDDEN AMISH SECRETS

DEBBY GIUSTI

LOVE INSPIRED SUSPENSE

INSPIRATIONAL ROMANCE

LOVE INSPIRED® SUSPENSE
INSPIRATIONAL ROMANCE

Recycling programs
for this product may
not exist in your area.

ISBN-13: 978-1-335-58112-9

Hidden Amish Secrets

Copyright © 2021 by Deborah W. Giusti

This edition published by arrangement with Harlequin Books S.A.

For questions and comments about the quality of this book, please contact us
at CustomerService@Harlequin.com.

Love Inspired
22 Adelaide St. West, 40th Floor
Toronto, Ontario M5H 4E3, Canada
www.Harlequin.com

Printed in U.S.A.

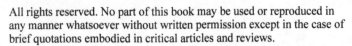

And be ye kind one to another, tenderhearted,
forgiving one another, even as God for Christ's sake
hath forgiven you.
—Ephesians 4:32

In memory of
Julianne Metz
August 29, 1935–February 10, 2020

A beautiful woman with sparkling eyes and a warm smile
who loved the Lord and spread joy wherever she went.

Thank you, Julie, for being not only a faithful reader
but also a dear friend.

ONE

Thunder rumbling overhead was as troubling as the guilt that still weighed heavily on Julianne Graber's heart even after five years. Losing her father and brother in one horrific night had been hard to accept. Having it ruled a murder-suicide made their passing even more tragic. The bishop's callous comment about *Gott*'s will had been the final blow. She had vowed never to return to her Amish home, yet here she was driving back to Mountain Loft, Georgia, on a stormy night that matched her mood.

The rain intensified, and wisps of fog impeded visibility. She lowered the headlights on her small Honda, activated the windshield wipers and checked the GPS on her smartphone. Her estimated time of arrival was close to midnight. She groaned and chastised herself, yet again, for leaving Dahlonega so late in the day.

Her upset increased as she glanced at the notice from the county authorities that was lying on the passenger seat. After reading the letter too many times, she could recite the words by heart.

Due to a rise in vagrancy and vandalism, buildings left unoccupied for more than five years will be considered abandoned unless efforts are made to either occupy or sell the property.

She wouldn't let conniving county bureaucrats lay claim to the farm, two-story house and outbuildings she had inherited from her father. Even if she didn't want to live there herself.

Over the last five years, she had learned to manage her grief and was better able to handle the memories of the hateful crime that had claimed her father's and brother's lives. Aunt Mary, her father's sister, had been her lifeline back to reality for the first two years. Eventually, needing to test her wings like a small bird leaving the nest,

Julie had abandoned her Amish faith, moved to a quaint college town in the North Georgia mountains and worked in a gift shop on the square in Dahlonega for the past three years. If not for the letter, she would be in her apartment getting ready for bed instead of navigating the twisting mountain road.

A curve appeared ahead. Easing down on the brake pedal, she hugged the shoulder as an approaching delivery truck in the opposite lane swerved around the bend. Frustrated by the aggressive driver, she laid on the horn, hoping to remind the trucker that speeding on the treacherous mountain road was anything but wise.

A rockslide had stopped traffic earlier and delayed her for more than two hours. She didn't want her arrival to be pushed back even later. Not that anyone expected her. The only welcome would come from an empty farmhouse and a row of graves on the hillside. Her father and brother were buried there, along with her mother, who had died a year earlier.

The road wound higher up the mountain

and eventually leveled into a plateau. A sign appeared on the left-hand side of the road:

Welcome to Mountain Loft, Established in 1840 by miners seeking their fortune in the Georgia Gold Rush.

She checked her speed and drove through the sleepy town, grateful the stoplights remained green and her progress was unencumbered.

In the daytime, she would see the Amish farm community that laid claim to the area west of town. This late at night, the farmers and their families were asleep in their beds, and their homes were bathed in darkness.

She passed her once-upon-a-time best friend's house. Rachel Hochstetler had driven Julianne home from the teen gathering at the lake the night her father and brother had died. With the memory of William Lavy's kiss still on her lips, Julie had entered her house to find her father lying in a pool of blood.

She grimaced at the memory and rubbed

her forehead, thinking again of the sharp inhale of breath she had heard behind her, along with her whispered name, before a hard object had slammed against her skull. After awakening hours later, she had stumbled to her feet and glanced at the far side of the room. Her brother, Bennie, sat propped against the wall, legs sprawled out in front of him. Mouth open. Eyes wide. She could still see the hole in his stomach and the gun clutched in his hand.

Tears burned her eyes and blurred her vision. She yanked a tissue from her purse, wiped it across her cheeks and pulled in a ragged breath as her father's house appeared in the distance. Correction—her house. Grateful that her Honda made better time than a horse-drawn buggy, she steeled her resolve, turned into the drive and braked to a stop near the back porch.

The rain had eased and the moon hung low in the sky, as it had that night so long ago. The sheriff had determined Bennie and her father had argued, and in a fit of anger, her brother had shot *Datt* and then turned the gun on himself. She still struggled to make sense of something so senseless.

Her mouth went dry, and a lump of grief filled her throat, but she was determined to face the past. Pulling in a fortifying breath, she grabbed her flashlight from the console, stepped from the car and climbed the back steps to the kitchen entrance.

Fisting her hand, she hesitated before keying open the door. The house was dark and silent as a tomb. She inhaled the stale air that wafted past her, half expecting the stench of pooled blood to fill her nostrils.

For a long, agonizing moment, she stood at the threshold, willing herself to step inside. A shrill, high-pitched scream replayed in her memory—her scream, when she'd finally regained consciousness and seen not only her father, but also her brother, dead. Heart pounding from the memory, she slammed the kitchen door and locked it with trembling hands. Morning would be soon enough to deal with the memories.

Needing to distance herself from the crime

scene that cut into her heart, she raced back to the safety of her car.

A twig snapped.

She stopped, cocked her ear and listened, her pulse pounding. Silence, except for the pitter-patter of raindrops falling from the trees. Relieved, she reached for the door handle.

Leaves rustled. Heart in her throat, she turned. A man dressed in black sprang from the darkness. A red bandana covered his face. He grabbed her arm and threw her to the ground.

"No!" She landed with a thud. Air sailed from her lungs. Gasping, she crawled to her knees and attempted to stand.

He thrust his leg forward and slammed his boot into her ribs.

She fell and clawed at the muddy drive.

Grasping her ankle with both hands, he dragged her toward the bushes. She thrashed and kicked her other leg.

His grip eased ever so slightly.

She kicked again. He groaned.

Again, she kicked. And again.

He tumbled backward.

Scrambling to her feet, she lunged for her car, opened the door and fell into the driver's seat. He reached for her and she slammed the door, catching the tips of his fingers. He screamed in pain and pounded his fist against the window.

She started the engine and floored the accelerator. The car fishtailed out of the drive. Yanking on the wheel, she turned onto the main road, heading toward Mountain Loft.

Her heart pounded nearly out of her chest. She had to get away. She glanced in the rearview mirror, her stomach rolling. Headlights followed after her onto the country road.

Her secondhand Honda wasn't built for speed. The man in black would overtake her before she got to town.

On the opposite side of the road, the Lavys' neighboring farm sat dark in the night. A narrow path behind the house led from the road to a stand of trees and a pond where her brother and William Lavy had played when they were young. If she could turn off the main road and hide near the pond, she might elude the attacker. She switched off her headlights, eased into the turn and bounced along the muddy path. The pond appeared ahead.

She stopped behind a cluster of pines, grabbed her phone and jumped from the car into a quagmire of mud. Pulling free, she stumbled toward the house and glanced at the main road just as a car raced by. All she saw was a flash of white.

Knowing he would turn around and come back to find her, she rounded the farmhouse, climbed the steps to the porch and pounded on the door.

"Mr. Lavy! Will! It's Julianne Graber. I need help."

She thought back five years to the morning she had fled in shock from her own house. William had been working in his barnyard. She had run toward him, tears streaming from her eyes.

"What's wrong, Julie?" he'd asked. "Tell me! What happened?"

"*Datt*... Bennie..." She'd gasped. "They're both dead."

Shoving aside the memory, she pounded on the door again.

Another sound came. She dropped her hand and listened. A car engine. Her pulse raced and her throat went dry. The man in the bandana was coming back.

She dashed around the side of the house as the white car pulled into the Lavys' drive. A lump filled her throat, but she fisted her hands, unwilling to cry. Ducking behind a large hedge, she held her breath. Her heart thumped so hard she was sure he could hear her.

His car door opened. He stepped to the drive. Through the branches of the shrubbery, she could see his pant legs and mud-caked boots.

A beam of light flickered from a flashlight. He turned it first to the porch and then toward the barn and outbuildings. Angling her gaze, she saw his black jacket and trousers. The bandana still covered his face. He hesitated for a long moment and then climbed into his car, backed onto the road and turned toward town. Driving slowly, he aimed the flashlight along the side of the road.

As he neared the path to the pond, she held her breath, fearing he would see tread marks in the mud. "Please," she whispered. "Keep driving."

The car eased to a stop. Light flickered over the path. Her heart nearly crashed through her chest. After what seemed like an eternity, he drove on.

Letting out the breath she was holding, she tapped 911 into her phone. Nothing. She checked her screen. No bars. Her stomach churned. She raced to her car and wanted to scream when she tried her cell again with the same result.

She needed to alert the sheriff's office. If her phone wouldn't work, she'd go there in person. Hunkered down in her car, she waited thirty minutes, giving the man in black time to arrive at his destination and be off the road. She turned the key in the ignition, relieved when the engine hummed to life, and stepped on the gas. A whirring sound filled the air as the tires spun in the soft mud.

With an audible moan, she got out, rounded to the rear of the car, placed her hands on the trunk and pushed with all her might. The car wouldn't budge, and all she succeeded in doing was sinking deeper into the mud. Her only option was to wait until morning.

She shivered, not only from the cold, but also from being attacked and having her car stuck. Her side ached, and her head felt like it would explode from stress. So much for a happy homecoming.

Something rustled in a nearby stand of trees.

After climbing quickly into her car, she hit the door lock button, scooted lower in the seat and narrowed her gaze, trying to discern what was roaming in the darkness. A fox or coyote perhaps? Brown bears were not uncommon in the mountains.

She blinked to bring the form into focus, but it disappeared from sight. Or had she imagined the movement altogether? One thing was certain—she would stay locked in the car until the first light of dawn.

Yanking a heavy lap blanket from the rear seat, she wrapped it around her shoulders and rested her head back. As the minutes passed, her eyes grew heavy. She snuggled into the blanket and closed her eyes.

The man with the red bandana who wanted to do her harm was the last thing she thought of before falling asleep, but it was William's face that filled her dream. She was at the lake so long ago. The moonlight broke through the trees and illuminated his searching eyes as he lowered his lips to hers.

Tap, tap, tap. The sound startled her and pulled her from her slumber. She opened her eyes to a glare of sunlight and blinked a blurred form into view.

A man stared down at her through the windshield. "Julianne?"

She rubbed her eyes and pulled herself upright, recognizing the angled face, full mouth and crystal-blue eyes.

William Lavy.

He was wearing an Amish jacket and a wide-brimmed felt hat.

"Is that you, Julie?"

She hadn't seen Will in five years, and until last night, she hadn't expected to see him again. She threw aside the blanket, adjusted her sweater and raked her hand through her hair, embarrassed he had found her asleep.

His brow was raised, and his mouth set in a frown as he continued to stare at her.

Pulling in a fragile breath, she offered him a weak smile.

"What happened? Are you okay?" His raised voice was filled with concern.

For half a heartbeat, she thought she was dreaming.

"Answer me, Jules. Are you okay?"

She tapped the button to lower the automatic window before realizing the car's engine was off. She grabbed the handle and pushed open the door.

The cold morning air swirled around her. "I must have—" Her sleep-laced tone was little more than a whisper, even to her own ears. She cleared her throat. "I must have fallen asleep."

"Looks like both you and your car got stuck in the mud." He leaned closer. "Are you okay?"

"I... I'm fine. A bit bruised, but—" Tears burned her eyes. She blinked them back.

"You're hurt." His gaze softened. "What happened?"

"I came home to sell my father's property." She glanced at the letter lying open on the console. "They want to take my farm. I left late in the day and then was delayed by a rockslide."

The words were tumbling out too fast, but she couldn't help herself. If she stopped talking, she might cry, and she was struggling to keep the tears at bay.

"When I got to my house," she continued without taking a breath, "a man in black wearing a red bandana was hiding in the bushes. He attacked me, then followed me in his car. I turned toward the pond, thinking you or your dad could help me."

Regret flashed in his eyes. "I was at a friend's wedding and spent the night. I saw your Honda when I returned this morning."

"Why would someone attack me?"

"Vandalism has become a problem." He gazed around, as if checking that the man in black wasn't hiding nearby. "That's why the authorities are concerned about unoccupied property, but vandals don't usually attack people."

She blinked back another rush of tears.

"Let's get your car out of the mud," he said. "Then we can drive to town and alert the sheriff. We can also stop at the medical clinic and have the doc make certain you're okay."

"I don't need a doctor, but I do need to talk to the sheriff."

"Start your car, Julie. I'll push from the rear. Give it a little gas when I signal you, but not too much."

She did as he asked and watched for his signal through the rearview mirror.

He stepped behind the car, placed his hands on the trunk and nodded. "Okay...now."

Julie pushed on the accelerator. The wheels spun.

Stepping to the side, William nodded again. "Put it in Reverse and ease it back, then forward."

Again, she followed his instructions. The car rolled back and she moved the gear to Drive. William pushed from the rear as she eased down on the accelerator. The wheels grabbed and the car broke free.

"Keep going," he called after her. "I'll meet you at the top of the hill."

Near the edge of the road, she pulled to a stop and waited for him there. Before meeting with the sheriff, she wanted to check her house to ensure the hateful man hadn't caused any damage last night. No one had known she was coming back to Mountain Loft, yet he'd been hiding in the bushes. What was he doing there, and why had he attacked her?

William hurried to the top of the hill to catch up to Julianne. She was spattered with mud, and fatigue lined her oval face, but he was drawn again to her beauty, just as he had been at the lake so long ago. Long auburn hair, jade-green eyes, arched eyebrows and an open expression that nearly took his breath away.

She leaned out the window as he approached her car. "Climb in. I want to stop at my house."

He glanced down at his boots. "If you don't mind a little mud."

"My shoes are caked. We can clean up at the pump."

He slid into the passenger seat. She exited onto the main road, drove the short distance to her farm and parked near the barn. They washed at the pump and wiped dry with a towel she had in her car.

After hanging the towel to dry, she stamped the mud from her shoes and then pointed to the shrubbery growing near the side of her house.

"The man was hiding there in the bushes last night. I—I didn't think I'd survive."

William searched the area she had indicated. "I don't see that he left anything behind."

"Except a few bruises that'll appear in a day or two." She rubbed her side and then turned her gaze to the farmhouse and stared at the structure for a long moment.

"I—I haven't been back since—"

He remained silent, giving her time to control the whirlwind of confusion evidenced by the arch of her neck and her furrowed brow.

She glanced around at the farm that had been her world for the first seventeen years of life. The house, the barn and outbuildings, the pastures in the distance and the fields were all dormant.

"It looks better than I expected," she admitted.

"I worked construction in Knoxville, and after I returned home last year, I shored up the fencing and completed some minor repairs around the place when I had free time," he explained.

Fresh tears filled her eyes. Evidently, she hadn't expected his help.

"*Danki*, William."

The Amish thank-you seemed to surprise her as much as the tears. She had left Mountain Loft before baptism and had undoubtedly worked hard to leave her Amish roots behind.

He touched her arm and she drew back ever so slightly, then pulled herself upright. "I didn't think coming home would be so hard."

"Don't go inside, Julie." His tone was firm, even to his own ears. "It's not necessary."

"I can't control the memories—" She steeled her jaw. "But facing the past in the light of day will help me heal even more."

He shook his head. "You need more time."

"It's been five years."

"A few more days won't hurt."

"Except I have a new life that's waiting for me." She stared at him, then turned to the porch and climbed the stairs.

A crow cawed and he glanced up as it soared overhead. Clouds blocked the sun and a cold wind whipped across the barnyard, tugging at Julianne's hair. With trembling hands, she slipped the key into the lock. The door creaked open. Straightening her shoulders, she entered the cold interior.

William wiped the mud from his boots and followed her inside, noting the simple furnishings, the woodstove, the oil lamps and kitchen cupboards. The curtains blocked the light and cast the house in shadows.

With decided steps, she approached the closest window, pushed back the curtain and peered through the dusty pane. She touched the glass, then turned and swept her gaze over the main room. "A good cleaning will help. Plus, I'll need supplies if I stay here."

"That's not wise after what happened last night. I have two spare guest rooms on the second floor. Both would provide for your privacy."

"And what would the town gossips say, William? Tongues would wag. I won't dishonor your name."

He smiled ruefully. "It would not be the first time people talked behind my back."

"Perhaps, but the bishop would take issue

with your father and insist he control his wayward son."

Evidently, she didn't know. "My father died five months ago."

"Oh, William." She clasped her hands over her heart. "I'm so sorry."

"I am, as well, but it is the way of life."

And death, which he failed to mention. Julianne knew enough about death.

"Now both of us are orphans, *yah*?" he said.

"I feel more like a teenager looking for what I left behind." She peered into the empty pantry.

His heart went out to her and he stepped closer. "Your aunt asked some of the ladies to clean the kitchen of anything perishable before she closed up the house."

"A wise decision." Julie tugged a strand of hair behind her ear. "I don't remember much about those first few weeks."

"The shock undoubtedly blocked your memory."

She touched the dusty counter and then

glanced up at him. "Aunt Mary said you tried to say goodbye."

"Yah." He pulled in a breath, seeing the question in her gaze. "I left Mountain Loft for a few years to find myself. My first stop was at your aunt's house in Willkommen. She said you were not ready to receive visitors."

"My aunt was protective." Julie sighed. "Perhaps overly so."

"She was thinking of your well-being."

"For which I am grateful. When I left Willkommen—"

He raised an eyebrow. "You're no longer staying with Mary?"

"I live in Dahlonega now."

"The old gold mining town?"

She nodded. "The site of the first major US gold rush in 1828."

He smiled. "You have become a history buff."

"Hardly, but the tourists have questions. They visit the mines and pan for gold and then buy gifts in the shop where I work."

Glancing at the *Englischer* clothing she

wore and the car parked in the drive, he voiced the question that begged to be asked. "Am I right to believe you are no longer Amish?"

"I decided to make a fresh start in Dahlonega. That included embracing *Englisch* ways." She angled her head and gazed at him with her jade-green eyes. "What about you? That night at the lake, you talked about leaving Mountain Loft. I presumed that meant leaving the faith as well."

"Living *Englisch* was my plan. Then my father became ill…" He shrugged. "Someone needed to care for him."

"Yet you struggled under his control when you were young."

"Young and foolish. We reconciled. His lungs were bad, and his well-being was more important than hanging on to past misunderstandings."

"You're a good man, William Lavy."

Her remark touched a chord. He didn't think of himself as *gut*, but he couldn't let his father languish alone. Julianne would have done the same if she'd been given the chance.

"The sheriff's never been one of my favorite people." She glanced around the kitchen and into the main room. "Especially the way he handled the investigation five years ago, but I need to report what happened last night, and I could use some support."

"I'll come with you. After we talk to the sheriff, we can stop at the Country Kitchen for waffles and coffee."

A hint of a smile tugged at her lips. "You remembered."

He remembered a lot of things about Julie that he needed to forget. Instead, he needed to focus on her safety. Someone had attacked her last night. William wanted to ensure the man in the red bandana didn't try to harm her again.

TWO

The last time Julie had seen Sheriff Paul Taylor had been following Bennie's and her dad's deaths. She hadn't liked him before then, and she'd liked him even less when he'd claimed the hateful crime was a murder-suicide.

Over the past five years, the sheriff had aged. His hair had grayed, his jaw hung slack and his eyes looked dull, as if he was less than enthusiastic about his job. Or maybe it was seeing Julianne again that troubled him.

"Have a seat, Ms. Graber." He motioned her toward one of the two chairs across from his desk and then glanced at William. "You, as well, Will."

Without mincing words or wasting time,

Julie got right to the point and explained what had happened.

"Did you recognize the assailant?" the sheriff asked.

She shook her head. "I saw his pant legs at one point. He was dressed in black trousers and a black jacket. A red bandana covered his face."

"Like a mask? Or a gaiter?"

No doubt seeing her confusion, he explained. "A gaiter is a tube scarf worn around the neck that can be pulled up to cover the nose and mouth and secured with elastic straps over the ears."

"I'm not sure about the elastic straps. All I saw was the bandana."

The sheriff eyed William for a long moment. "Was he dressed Amish?"

"I don't think so, yet the night was dark," she admitted.

"There was a moon last night," the sheriff countered.

"Which went behind a heavy blanket of clouds." She stood her ground. "I didn't get a sense that he was Amish. Plus, he was driving a car and not a buggy."

"Yet we know Amish kids drive their *Englisch* friends' cars." The sheriff glanced at William again and then back at her. "What can you tell me about the vehicle?"

"It was white. That's all I know. I was hiding behind a bush when he approached William's house. I didn't want to make any noise, so I stood still and never got a good view of him or his car."

"Any reason someone would want to do you harm, Ms. Graber?"

"That's what I need you to find out, Sheriff. I came home to sell my farm and don't plan to be here long. The last thing I expected was a welcoming committee of one."

He chuckled.

She bristled. "Did I miss the joke?"

"No, ma'am."

The sheriff grabbed a pen from his desk drawer and jotted something on a notepad. "Where are you staying in case I need to get in touch with you?"

"At my father's house."

He pursed his lips. "There's a motel on the road to Amish Mountain."

"I'm aware of the motel." Why squander money renting a room when she had a house that would provide for her needs? "I'll stay at the farm in case a buyer wants to see the property."

"We've had an influx of vagrants around these parts." He tapped his pen against the notepad. "They bed down in abandoned houses and steal anything they can sell for money or drugs. This guy seems more focused. You need to be careful. He might return."

Julie had known coming home would be unsettling, but she hadn't expected to be attacked. "So you think it's someone passing through town?"

The sheriff shrugged. "Hard to say. We'll keep our eyes open. I'll let you know if we come up with a suspect. You'll press charges, right?"

"If you find him. It doesn't sound like you have any leads."

"I feel certain someone will turn up. Could be a newcomer who likes true crime."

"I don't understand."

"A murder-suicide in an abandoned house might attract a certain type of person."

She didn't like his reference. "You mean a criminal who likes to attack women?"

"I'm just saying, the lure of the old Graber farmhouse could have drawn him."

"For the record, the house is no longer standing vacant. I'm living there, and I'll protect my property in whatever way I can."

He chuckled again. "I hear ya."

She wanted the sheriff to do more than hear her. She wanted him to find the man who had done her harm. "I'll stop by your office the next time I'm in town. Hopefully, you'll have information about the vagrant or true-crime enthusiast. Either way, he needs to be apprehended before he strikes again."

William understood Julianne's frustration as they left the sheriff's office.

"Sheriff Taylor's attitude hasn't improved," she said with a huff. "Maybe I'm biased, but he seems even less enthusiastic about his job."

"He's ready to retire, although you lit a fire under his feet. Stopping back in a couple days will be a good idea. He might have something by then."

"I hope so."

"Let's get breakfast." William pointed to the diner farther down the street.

The inviting smell of fried eggs, sausages and coffee wafted past them as they stepped into the busy restaurant. The majority of the customers were townspeople enjoying a hearty meal, with a smattering of Amish folks sprinkled into the mix.

"There's a table in the corner." William ushered her through the crowd and held her chair as she sat with her back to the wall.

An Amish girl approached them carrying a coffeepot in hand. "What can I get you folks?"

"Two orders of waffles and coffee for us." He looked at Julianne. "How 'bout some eggs and hash browns, too?"

"Just waffles and coffee for me," she said as the waitress filled their mugs.

William's stomach growled. He'd been up since dawn and hadn't eaten. "Hash browns on the side for me and eggs over easy."

"I'll get that order in right away." The waitress hurried back to the kitchen.

Julianne blew into the mug and took a sip of the hot brew. "Thanks for suggesting breakfast. You knew what I needed."

He chuckled. "Selfishly, I was thinking of my own hunger. I know my way around a kitchen, but I take advantage of any opportunity to eat someone else's cooking."

"You live alone, right?"

He nodded. Her question seemed to have a deeper meaning. He took a long pull from his mug to give her time to explore what she really wanted to ask.

"I—I thought you would be married by now." She offered him a crooked smile that caused his chest to tighten. Her green eyes held his gaze. "You always were a ladies' man, Will."

"I'm not sure that's a compliment."

"Sorry." She placed her mug on the table. "I didn't mean anything negative. It's just that many of the local girls had their eyes on you."

"Looking back, I regret that my focus was somewhat skewed in my youth."

Her smile warmed his heart.

"We—" The smile faded. She blinked back the tears that filled her eyes. "We all made mistakes."

Almost five years had passed, yet her pain still seemed so raw. "Bennie was a *gut* person, Julie. No matter what the sheriff's investigation ruled."

She swallowed hard. "I'm to blame."

He reached for her hand to offer support. "How can you say that?"

"Did Bennie not tell you what I did?" She pulled back her hand.

"Only that your father forbade either of you from seeing me."

Nodding ever so slightly, she added, "*Datt* said you were a bad influence."

He tried to smile. "You didn't seem to think that when we were at the lake."

"Foolishly, I told *Datt* that you and Bennie planned to meet later that night." She took a deep breath. "He must have been waiting for Bennie when he came home. They argued..."

She bit her lip, and her hands trembled as she raised the mug.

He needed to set her straight. "But Bennie and I didn't meet that night, Julianne."

"Exactly." She pointed a finger at her chest. "Because you were with me, William. That was my ploy to keep you from him."

A weight settled on his shoulders. "You flirted with me at the lake to keep me from meeting your brother? So Bennie would not disobey your father's orders?"

"It sounds foolish, doesn't it?" She almost laughed. No doubt seeing his confusion, she tilted her head. "Is something wrong?"

"Nothing is wrong." His tone was sharper than he'd intended. "Besides, it happened long ago."

He straightened, unwilling for her to see his upset. "Bennie and I didn't plan to meet that night," he repeated to ensure she heard him correctly. "He was with Emma. I was..."

William refused to say that he'd been interested in spending time with Julie. She'd seemed interested as well, but she'd used him that night to protect her brother. He also didn't say that in the last five years he hadn't thought of courting or taking a wife because other women paled in comparison to Julianne.

"William, I..." She hesitated as if wanting to apologize for her comment.

When she failed to continue, he realized she could not backtrack from the truth even if she wanted to make him feel better.

The waitress appeared, seemingly from thin air, probably because he had been so focused on Julie and what she had revealed.

"More coffee?" she asked, placing the loaded plates in front of them. Without waiting for a reply, she refilled their mugs.

William was no longer hungry. He picked at his food and paid the bill as soon as Julia placed her fork on the table and wiped her mouth on the napkin. She had eaten little.

Both of them seemed to have lost their appetites.

"I need to buy some groceries," she said as they walked toward the door.

Glad for something to talk about other than the past, Will nodded. "Harvey Jones still runs the only grocery store in town."

"How's he doing?"

"You know Harvey. A friend to all."

"And Mrs. Jones?"

"Nancy's about the same. She has good days and bad days. I doubt she will ever get over her daughter's death."

"She doted on Anna. We were good friends, but I must admit to being a little envious. I wanted to wear her fancy *Englisch* clothes and have colorful bows in my hair."

"That's typical for a young Amish girl."

"My *mamm* said it was prideful. She wanted me to stop seeing Anna."

"Like your father wanted you to stop seeing me."

She glanced up at him. He saw something in her gaze that made him wonder if she felt as confused as he did.

The door pushed open, and Mose Miller stormed inside, nearly knocking over Julianne.

"Watch where you're going." William caught her arm to keep her from stumbling backward. "Apologize to the lady."

Mose was big and bulky, and liked to shove his weight around, which wasn't a good attribute for an Amish guy. Some said he was a powder keg waiting to explode.

"Get outta my way," he snarled at William and then turned and nodded to Julianne. "Pardon me, ma'am. I hope I didn't hurt you."

His tone was less than sincere, and something about the way he glared at Julianne made William think about the man who had attacked her. He glanced down and saw scratches on Mose's hand and a bandage around his index finger.

"Who was that?" Julie asked.

"Mose Miller. He married Emma Yoder."

"Bennie's girlfriend?"

Will nodded. "They married a couple years after your brother's death. They have a baby on the way. The talk in town is that Mose hopes to buy his own land to farm before their child's birth. Right now, they're living with his parents on thirty-five acres closer to town."

"I'm sorry for Emma."

"A lot of folks in town feel the same way."

If Julianne left Mountain Loft without selling her property, the county could take the farm and dispose of the land at auction, well below the market price.

Will glanced back and caught Mose's gaze as he sat at the table they had just vacated. Mose wanted his own land, and he was known for getting what he wanted. Will didn't like the thoughts that kept popping through his head.

As the sheriff had mentioned, an Amish guy could borrow a car—a white car—from an *Englischer* friend, but if so, would he try to frighten a woman off her land? Would he kick her and attempt to drag her into the bushes?

William's gut tightened. How far would a man like Mose go to acquire his own farm?

THREE

Stepping into the grocery store brought back more memories that tugged on Julianne's heart. She saw the plaque on the wall that hung below the crossed mining picks: Jones Grocery, 1828. Harvey Jones traced his lineage to the store's first owner, who had served the early miners searching for gold. A map on the wall showed the site of the mine that had been in his family for generations.

Bennie had stocked shelves here as a young teen and had managed the store in the evenings when he was older. She could still see him standing behind the counter, laughing at the jokes some of the old Amish farmers would tell.

Mr. Jones, wearing an apron over a navy button-down collared shirt and khaki slacks, stood with his back to the door and turned as she entered. The look of surprise that crossed his face brought a smile to her lips.

"Why, Julianne Graber, you bring a bit of sunshine to this old man's day."

Her heart warmed at his remark. "I won't hear of you saying old, but it's good to see you, Mr. Jones."

He playfully wagged his finger. "Now, now, dear girl, you're an adult and old enough to call me Harvey like everyone else in town. What brings you back to Mountain Loft?"

William followed her inside. Harvey nodded a perfunctory greeting.

"I need to sell my family farm," Julianne admitted as she grabbed a shopping cart.

"I saw a copy of the letter the county mailed out." Harvey shook his head. "Hard enough to come back after what happened. Even harder when you have to deal with bureaucrats."

"The good thing is that selling the property will bring closure," she insisted.

"Of course, it will." He thought for a moment. "There's a new B and B in town. Is that where you're staying? Or did you get a room at the motel on the mountain road?"

"I need to stay at the farm so I can go through my *datt*'s things and be available if buyers want to look at the house."

He pursed his full lips and thought for a moment. "Let me handle the sale of your property, Julianne. It's the least I can do as close as you and Anna were growing up. You don't need to upset yourself going home again. I'll let you know about any interested buyers. I can send the necessary documents to you wherever you're living if a deal comes in."

She appreciated his thoughtfulness. "I have an apartment in Dahlonega, but I'm here now and plan to see this through."

His gaze warmed. "Your father would be proud of you."

Although Harvey meant well, his comment was like a slap to her face. How could her father be proud of her after she had tattled on her brother, thinking he had arranged to meet with William that night?

Not that she'd thought Bennie would ever kill their *datt*, but he must have felt threatened, since he had his gun in hand. No doubt, their heated argument had escalated into something neither of them could have foreseen.

William touched her arm. "You have groceries to purchase."

Grateful that he had steered her back to the purpose of their visit, she nodded and pushed the shopping cart down the aisle.

"Can I help you find anything?" Harvey asked.

"Unless you've reorganized the shelves, I should be able to locate everything I want." She placed a pound of coffee in her cart, then continued to gather the other items she would need for the few days she planned to stay in Mountain Loft.

The bell over the door rang. Julianne turned to see Deacon Abraham Schwartz enter. A tall man with a gray beard and pointed nose, he and her father had been friends.

"Morning, Abe," Harvey called out. "I've got your order ready."

The deacon smiled, but when he noticed Julianne, his face soured. He glanced at Harvey and shook his head. "Hold it for me, Harvey. I'll return later."

The sting of rejection pulled at her heart, and she hurried through the rest of her shopping. She had never been baptized and therefore had never been shunned in the full sense of the word for leaving her faith, but anyone who turned *fancy* wasn't exactly welcome within the Amish community.

"Don't forget ice if you want to use your *datt*'s refrigerator," William suggested.

She didn't know if Will understood the significance of the deacon's hasty retreat, but she was grateful to focus on needing to keep perishable items cold instead of on Abe Schwartz's obvious snub.

"Thanks for reminding me. I've gotten used to having electricity." She had gotten used to a lot of things over the last three years. Living Amish might prove to be a challenge.

After she had paid for the groceries, the door to the store opened again, and Mrs. Jones stepped inside. She was tall and slender with big green eyes, just like Anna.

Seeing Julianne, she gasped. Confusion flashed in her troubled gaze.

With her heart aching for the still-grieving mother, Julie stepped closer. "Mrs. Jones, do you recognize me?"

The older woman blinked back tears. "How could I not, Julianne? Although for a moment with your long hair, I thought…"

She had thought her own daughter, Anna, was standing before her. People had often commented the girls could be twins as they'd played in front of the grocery.

"I told Julianne she should stay at the B and B in town or the motel on the mountain road," Harvey said from behind the counter.

"Or you could stay with us, dear," Mrs. Jones offered.

Which would only unsettle the fragile woman even more. "Thank you, but as I told Harvey, there's work to be done at home before I sell the farm."

"Yes, dear, of course, but you must come again soon."

"I will, for sure." After saying goodbye, she and Will gathered the groceries in their arms and headed to the car.

"Mrs. Jones was having one of her good days," Will said as he opened the trunk of the car. "The roads were icy that night, but she still blames herself."

Guilt was a heavy burden to carry. Julianne knew that all too well. Anna had died when the car Mrs. Jones was driving went off the road. The long-grieving mother couldn't forgive herself.

Julianne understood grief. She had lost too many people she loved. Perhaps that's why she had left the Amish community and isolated herself in the *Englisch* world. Folks in Dahlonega were friendly, but they were slow to open their hearts and their homes to a young woman new to town. Three years, and she only had a handful of friends. Probably because of her desire to keep her distance. If she got close, she would have to share her story. Some things were better left unsaid.

William knew her past, but he wasn't a threat. Plus, she was grateful for his help. Her aunt had mused that William might have been involved in what happened that night, but Julianne knew better. He had been with her at the lake until she'd hitched a ride home with Rachel Hochstetler.

By then, her father was dead. And her brother?

If Bennie had been dead, why had she heard the door in the kitchen close behind her?

William finished loading the groceries in Julie's car and closed the trunk. "Where to now?"

"Do you mind if I stop at Mountain Real Estate?" Julianne asked.

"Not a problem. Brad Abbott moved his office to the end of the next block."

They parked in front of the real-estate building and climbed from the car. William held the door for Julianne and followed her inside.

Gloria Davenport, the blond receptionist, smiled as he entered. "How are you, William? It's been a long time."

He nodded. Gloria had snuck out of her house to meet him at the lake a few times when they were young.

"You remember Julianne Graber." He motioned to Julie.

The receptionist forced a smile. "Brad said you wanted to talk to him about selling your farm. I'll tell him you're here." She rose from the desk and hurried to an office farther down the hall.

"Didn't I hear a rumor about you and Gloria?" Julia said with a smirk.

"We were friends."

"Very good friends from what I heard."

"People talk. They don't always tell the truth."

She nodded. "You're right."

Gloria hurried back and pointed to the office she had just left. "Brad said he'll see you now."

The last thing William wanted was to make small talk with Gloria. "I've got an errand to run. I'll meet you at your car, Jules."

The door opened, and a big guy wearing muddy work boots and a black fleece jacket stepped inside. He looked at William and frowned, then stared at Gloria.

"What's going on, babe?"

"Nothin', Ralph. These folks are here to talk to Brad."

He glanced again at William. "You sure about that?"

"Actually, I was just leaving," William said.

Ralph Reynolds had grown up in the mountains with an alcoholic dad and four brothers who all had a penchant for trouble. Two were in jail. The youngest brother was addicted to meth. The family's track record wasn't good. William had heard Gloria was seeing Ralph. In William's opinion, he was a bad apple from a rotten tree, and Gloria deserved better.

After nodding farewell, Will hurried outside. The errand he had mentioned was actually a call he needed to make. Gloria would have let him use the office phone, but he wanted to distance himself from the past and from a seemingly jealous boyfriend who had jumped to the wrong conclusion.

The words of wisdom from his father had proved true. "You reap what you sow," his father had told him more than once. If only Will could go back in time and relive his youth.

"*Gott*, forgive me," Will said as he hurried to the phone booth.

Once he had completed his call, he waited by Julie's Honda. "How did it go?" he asked as she left the office and neared the car.

"He's coming by tomorrow to look over the property. We'll talk selling price then."

"Did he say how the market is?"

"The *Englischers* aren't buying much in the area, but the Amish often want to move here from other locations. He'll place an ad in *The Budget* newspaper, which could attract a buyer, but first he wants to see the property and the house. Thanks for keeping the place looking good, William."

"It's the least I could do."

She stared at him as if confused by his comment.

The least he could do because he hadn't taken her home that night. If he had, she wouldn't have entered the house alone. He still didn't believe Bennie had knocked her out.

Bennie and Julie had had their spats as siblings, but they'd loved one another. Bennie wouldn't have hurt his sister, yet someone had. If not Bennie, then who?

Before Julianne backed out of the parking space, the sheriff flagged them down. "I've got good news."

"You caught the man who attacked me?" she asked.

"The deputy's bringing him in as we speak. I'll question him and hold him overnight. Stop by tomorrow, and we can draw up those charges."

"You're confident he's the one?"

"Almost one hundred percent. Rest easy tonight, Ms. Graber."

"That is good news," Julia said to William as they headed out of town.

Good news if the sheriff's assumption panned out. William thought of the miners who had flocked to Mountain Loft hoping to strike it rich. They had all been optimistic, yet for most of them, their dreams had never come true.

Julianne wanted the attacker to be apprehended. William did, as well, but the sheriff was known for taking shortcuts. With Julianne's safety in question, William wanted to ensure the real attacker had been detained before he let down his guard.

FOUR

William was uneasy about leaving Julie alone at her farm. He carried her groceries inside, placed the ice in the cooling tray of the refrigerator and brought in wood for her stove. After starting the fire, he asked if he could do anything else to help her.

She expressed her thanks but seemed ready for him to leave. Perhaps she needed time alone to adjust to the house and the memories. Still, his heart went out to her. Determined though she was to sell the farm, he feared she had a fragile underpinning that could easily crack under duress.

Later that night, when the chores were done, he walked back to her house. Just as he turned into the drive, he heard the clip-clop of a horse's hooves approaching on the road from town. As William watched, Mose

Miller passed by in his buggy. He kept his eyes on his mare and flicked his whip to speed the horse along the narrow road that led to the lake.

William had heard him berating Emma on more than one occasion and had stepped in to offer his assistance a few weeks ago, which was probably why Mose's temper had flared earlier today at the Country Kitchen.

Will watched the buggy until it disappeared from sight, then he hurried toward Julianne's house and knocked on the door.

"It's Will," he called out, hoping to allay any concern she might have about a visitor this late in the day. The sun sat on the horizon and darkness would soon fall.

She opened the door, her hair a bit disheveled, and stared at him as if surprised by his visit.

"I—I thought..." What had he thought? That she would be visibly grieving and would need his support?

"I wanted to ensure your lamps worked," he quickly explained. "And that you had enough oil."

Her gaze softened. "Thank you, William. I filled them this afternoon and tested them. The wicks burned, and the light was bright."

"What about the woodstove? Do you have enough wood?"

"I have ample wood, thanks to your thoughtfulness earlier."

"You will lock your doors?" He didn't want to unduly frighten her, but they were some distance from town, and until he knew for sure, her attacker could still be on the loose.

She nodded. "A habit I started when I moved to Dahlonega. I'm not concerned about staying alone."

Perhaps she should be.

"Remember what the sheriff said, Will. I feel confident the man in black is spending tonight and hopefully many nights in the future in custody."

He hoped that was the case, but—

"Just be careful, Julianne." He glanced around her into the kitchen. "Is there anything I can do?"

"Don't worry. That's what you can do. I'm

not the teenager who needed help five years ago."

Her comment pricked him like the tip of a sharp knife. "I can see that, Julie."

"I've lived on my own without problem," she continued. Then, as if realizing his upset, her tone mellowed. "Although I'm grateful for your thoughtfulness. Thank you for checking on me."

He smelled coffee and wished she would invite him inside.

"Well..." He turned and gazed at the sun, low in the sky. An ominous dread he couldn't explain settled over him. "If you need anything, I'll be right down the road."

"I'm fine, William."

"Then I'll see you tomorrow."

She shut the door and turned the lock.

He stood for a few seconds staring at the closed door and thinking of the many times he had stopped by the Graber home in his youth to see Bennie. One winter day, he had taken closer notice of Julie. She seemed to have changed overnight. From then on, he had considered her more than his friend's kid sister.

Not long after that, his relationship with his father had become even more volatile, and a desire to break away from Amish control made him search for new ways to assert his independence. He had borrowed an *Englisch* friend's car and had driven too fast along the mountain road, as if to prove his worth. He'd crashed the car, but had walked away from the accident. When Bennie's *datt* learned about William's reckless actions, he was no longer welcome in the Graber home.

Leaving the porch, he hurried to the road. The sun would set before long. He wished his own internal upheaval would set, as well.

As he walked home, thoughts of Julianne returned unbidden, transporting him back to the night at the lake when he had taken her in his arms. Her softness had made his breath catch and his heart nearly stop beating. The clouds had parted in the sky, and a narrow band of moonlight had broken through the branches of the trees to illuminate her face, which had been turned up to him with eager anticipation. What he saw in her gaze had made everything in his life up to that moment fade away.

He had driven his buggy home long after Julie had left him at the lake. His heart had longed to knock on her kitchen door so he could see her again, never realizing what had happened to her inside.

Early the next morning, he had caught sight of her running down the road, her *kapp* gone, and her long auburn hair flying in the wind. As she drew closer, he'd seen her tears and swollen cheeks and the fear that filled her gaze.

If only he could step back in time and stop the tragedy before it happened, but life moved on, and second chances were hard to come by.

Julianne's brother had been a great guy who'd had his whole future ahead of him. He had planned to court Emma and wanted to ask her to marry him once he'd saved money from his job at Jones Grocery so they had something with which to start their life together.

But Bennie's life had been snatched away too soon.

His friend never would have shot his father and taken his own life. Bennie wasn't a killer, no matter what the sheriff claimed.

After William's surprise visit, Julia kept thinking of the handsome farmer as she studied her now tidy house. Dust had settled everywhere over the years, and she had spent the afternoon cleaning. With a damp cloth, she'd wiped down the furnishings until the rich wood gleamed. She'd found the broom in the utility room and had swept the floor, then mopped it and tossed the dirty water outside. The kitchen had been the last area to tackle. She'd wiped the cabinets and countertops and had felt a sense of satisfaction when she hung the wet rag to dry.

Peering through the kitchen window as the last light of day slipped below the horizon, she saw the pasture where their horses used to graze. The farm animals had been sold and the money placed in a bank account.

She had used some of the funds to buy her car and a few items for her apartment.

Working at the gift shop covered her expenses but left little at the end of the month. Even if she sold the farm, the taxes would be steep. Plus, she needed a way to support herself long-term, a job that would provide health-care insurance and some type of retirement pension. Her aunt had suggested teaching, but she had no formal education beyond the eighth grade. That level of study, along with the many books she had read to increase her knowledge, would suffice if she taught at an Amish school, but she wasn't willing to remain in Mountain Loft. Not that the community would be interested in hiring an *Englischer* to teach their children.

She looked back at the stained floor next to the stairs, her heart pounding with the memory it evoked. Grabbing the braided rag rug from the front entryway—the rug had been made by her mother—she placed it over the stain and breathed out a sigh of relief.

Her stomach growled with hunger and she

realized she hadn't eaten since breakfast. She poured a cup of coffee, made a sandwich and ate it standing at the counter as she continued to gaze out the window. In the distance, she could see William's farm and the faint glow of light in a downstairs window. She was grateful for his concern and appreciated that he had checked on her earlier in the evening.

Things could have been so different, if only—

Not willing to dwell on the past, she swallowed the last of the sandwich, wiped her mouth on a napkin and dropped it in the trash.

A small desk sat in the main room, where her father used to do his ledgers, adding the cost of feed and equipment and balancing the outlay against the money earned through the sale of cattle and seasonal crops.

She ran her hand over the desk's smooth wooden surface as she settled into the desk chair. His papers were still in the drawer. She rifled through the forms, noting his tight script and perfect penmanship.

He had been meticulous in his record keeping. As she studied the ledgers, she realized the farm had prospered, yet the bank-account statements she'd received after his death had been modest at best.

In the bottom drawer, she found an envelope. She pulled it out and stared at her mother's name written in her father's hand. Strange that he would keep a note he had addressed to her, unless he had forgotten about it after her death.

Julianne removed a sheet of unlined paper from the envelope and leaned closer to the oil lamp.

Dearest Margaret,
Should any harm befall me, remember the money I have set aside for our older years. I know you will make good use of it, and I hope with time, the amount will grow. Also, the cash kept here at the house will be available immediately so you can provide for the children until the other funds are available. The community will rally to help you, but you

may need more than they have to offer. This note is not to make you worry. It is to bring comfort should Gott call me home first. Stay in His care and trust in Him to provide for your needs.

Your loving husband, Daniel

Reading the note again, her eyes focused on his mention of available cash. Aunt Mary had taken care of shutting down the farm after his death, but she had never mentioned finding a stash of money. Throughout that time, Julianne had remained sequestered at her aunt's house in Willkommen and had never set foot in her childhood home again. Until this morning.

The day had been long and stressful, and Julianne suddenly felt overcome with fatigue. Tomorrow would be time enough to search for the missing money. She slipped the note into the envelope and clutched it in her hand as she climbed the stairs.

Her room was the same as when she had left it, except for the bedding that had been washed, stored in a protective plastic case and placed in a drawer. Grateful to have clean linens, she made the bed, changed into the sleepwear she had brought and slipped into bed.

In her youth, she had prayed before going to sleep. Something she had not done for years. Settling her head on the pillow, she wondered if she would ever call on *Gott* again.

Her eyes were heavy, and she started to drift into a light slumber. Thoughts of William circled through her mind like a dream not yet formed.

A clap of thunder startled her awake. She blinked her eyes open and stared into the darkness. Outside, strong gusts of wind rustled in the trees. The boughs of the hardwoods creaked and groaned.

Her pulse picked up a notch as another sound filtered through the night. Lying perfectly still, she tilted her head and strained to distinguish the subtle nuances of what she had heard.

A rhythmic *pat, pat, pat.*

Or were her ears playing tricks on her?

Another rumble of thunder, then a loud crash, as if the barn door had blown open. She jumped out of bed, hurried to the window and stared at the farmyard below. The barn was secure, but the door to her father's workshop swung back and forth in the wind. Relieved to learn the source of the crash, she let out the breath she was holding, slipped into her robe and headed downstairs.

Much as she wanted to remain inside, the wind could blow the door off its hinges. If what the sheriff had said was true, last night's attacker was under lock and key. It was doubtful anyone else would be prowling around, especially in the middle of a raging storm. If she ran to the workshop, quickly closed the door and made sure it was secure, she could return to the comfort of the warm house within minutes.

She grabbed her coat off the wall peg and slipped it on before she opened the kitchen door and stared into the night, searching for a man in black lurking in the shadows. Seeing nothing that caused her concern, she pulled in a breath and raced into the storm.

The wind tugged at her hair and rain stung her cheeks. She lowered her head and ran toward the small outbuilding.

Stepping inside, she surveyed her father's workbench and the tools hanging on the wall pegs. His shop was usually neat and organized, which was her father's way in everything he did, but tonight, the small area was cluttered with tools strewn helter-skelter over his workbench.

Something moved behind her. A mouse or—

She glanced over her shoulder and into eyes glaring at her over the top of a red bandana. Her heart nearly stopped, then a jolt of adrenaline shoved her forward. She raced out of the shop and across the yard.

Footsteps sounded behind her.

Forcing her legs to move faster, she slipped on the wet grass, nearly tripping, then righted herself and hurried on.

He grabbed her arm. She screamed and jerked from his hold. He tugged at her coat and ripped it from her shoulders.

She kept running. Her feet splashed

through puddles of water. Wet strands of hair plastered against her face, and her heart pounded nearly out of her chest.

The door to the house—had she left it open? She flew up the porch steps and into the kitchen. Slamming the door, she turned the lock.

The house shook in the bellowing storm and thrashing wind. She dashed to the stairs. The doorknob rattled behind her.

She glanced back. A dark form stood staring through the window. Holding back the scream that welled up within her, she raced upstairs to her bedroom, grabbed her cell phone off the nightstand and tapped in 911, grateful she had a signal.

A Southern voice drawled a greeting. "You've reached 911. State your emergency."

"Someone attacked me last night. He came back… He's at my door. This is Julianne Graber." Breathless, she provided her address. "I'm alone and need help."

"I'll contact the sheriff's office. Stay on the line."

She couldn't wait on Dispatch. She needed to do something. Now!

Think, think. How could she protect herself?

Her father's hunting rifle.

She ran into his room, peered under his bed and pulled out the rifle. Dropping the lever, she checked the chamber and magazine. Both were empty.

Where was the ammunition?

Trembling, she opened one dresser drawer, then another and another. She fisted her hands and wanted to scream with frustration.

Finally, she yanked open the bottom drawer and felt into the deep recesses. Her fingers found the cardboard box. She pulled it out, fumbled with the lid and nearly dropped the cartridges as she loaded them into the rifle.

She dashed to the window and opened it ever so slightly. The night air blew into the room, chilling her. Footsteps raced across the drive, but she saw nothing in the darkness. Her mouth went dry and her ears roared.

He was running away. A swell of relief fluttered through her. Then another sound came from below.

Bam, bam, bam.

Her heart lurched. He hadn't run away after all.

Still clutching the rifle, she retraced her steps and crept down the stairs. Every nerve in her body pinged, like an elastic band stretched tight. A large form stood on the porch, his fisted hand pounding on the kitchen window so hard she expected it to break.

Her heart nearly stopped. She hugged the wall and watched the huge bulk of him press his face against the glass. With trembling hands, she raised the rifle to her shoulder, knowing he would gain entrance to the house at any moment. She needed to be ready to defend herself. She also needed to be strong and remain calm, although the thought of shooting someone, even in self-defense, made her tremble even more.

Again, he peered through the window. Mustering her courage, she placed her thumb on the hammer. Her breath caught. The hammer stuck and failed to cock. She tried again, then again.

He jiggled the doorknob and pounded on the window. In the blink of an eye, he would crash through the door. Terror filled her. The rifle was useless, and there was no other way she could defend herself.

Tree branches thrashed against the house. The roar of the rain hitting the tin roof echoed in her ears. Through the din, another sound made her tilt her head and listen.

Sirens screamed in the distance. Law enforcement was on the way, but they wouldn't arrive in time. Hot tears burned her eyes. She glanced at the rag rug covering the bloodstain at the foot of the stairs. Her father and brother had died violently in this room.

"Oh, *Gott*, don't let me die like them."

FIVE

Lights flashed as the sheriff's sedan raced toward the farm, filling William with relief but also concern about what Julianne would do until law enforcement arrived.

"Lower the rifle, Jules." He kept his voice even and his gaze focused on where she stood in the open doorway with the rifle on her shoulder and her finger poised on the trigger.

She looked like a spooked mare, wild and dangerous. Coming back to Mountain Loft had been hard. She had admitted as much earlier, and whatever had happened tonight seemed to have sent her into a tailspin.

"The prowler ran away," he told her, his voice calm and consoling. "You no longer need to worry, Julie."

"Stay where you are, Will."

He heard the tremble in her voice and saw the fear in her eyes. "Everything's okay," he soothed. "Law enforcement's here. They'll make sure no one hurts you."

The scream of the siren ended abruptly as the squad car turned into the drive, and the flash of lights played over the side of the house. She turned toward the car as the driver's door opened. A deputy climbed from behind the wheel, weapon in hand. He was tall and slender, midtwenties, with deep set eyes that moved from Julie to William and back to Julie again.

"I'm Deputy Sheriff Terence O'Reilly, ma'am. You can lower that rifle and place it on the floor of the porch, nice and easy."

"I—I didn't think you'd get here in time." She glanced down as if only now realizing the rifle was in her hands.

"Lower the rifle, ma'am."

"Yes, of course." Slowly, she stooped and placed the weapon at her feet. "The trigger jammed," she explained as she stood upright. "It wouldn't have worked even if I had wanted to fire a round."

"Step away from the rifle, ma'am." The deputy's voice was firm but not threatening.

She nodded and moved to the side of the doorway.

"You want to tell me what happened, ma'am?" O'Reilly asked, his weapon trained on Julianne.

She looked confused as she glanced at William and then at the officer. Swallowing hard, she squared her shoulders and seemed to have a surge of determination as she declared, "You can put away your gun, Deputy. The only firearm I had was my father's rifle."

"Yes, ma'am. That's good to know." O'Reilly hesitated a moment, then holstered his weapon, climbed the porch steps and retrieved the rifle. "So how did all this start?"

"Start?" Julianne glanced again at William. "I heard sounds, like footsteps. The door to my father's workshop slammed in the wind." She pointed to the small outbuilding. "I planned to secure the door, but I found a man wearing a bandana-type mask hiding in the shop. He ran after me. Somehow, I managed to get back to the house and locked the door behind me. He rattled the knob and then pounded on the window. I feared it would break."

O'Reilly glanced at William. "Did you go into the workshop?"

"No, sir. The man was on the porch when I arrived. He fled. I lost him in the woods and came back to check on Julie."

Will pointed to his own farm. "I live across the road. When the storm hit, I was concerned about Julianne. She came back to Mountain Loft last night and was accosted here on her property. I accompanied her to town today when she talked to the sheriff. He suspected a vagrant and said the man was in custody. I was worried the guy might return and wanted to make sure Julianne was okay."

"So you banged on the door and scared her into getting her father's rifle?" the deputy asked.

"If I'd had a phone, I would have called her." William heard the irritation in his own voice.

"Did this man cause you any harm or distress?" the deputy asked Julianne as he pointed to William.

She stared at him. "I—I thought..." Then with a definitive shake of her head, she sighed. "No, he frightened the prowler away."

William didn't know if she believed what she told the deputy, but he was grateful she had corroborated his story. He'd had a bad reputation as a teen, and some people had a hard time forgetting the mistakes he had made in his youth. He recognized O'Reilly from his younger years, and although they'd never run in the same circles, rumors had a penchant for living on in Mountain Loft, and Will didn't want his past to cause him problems tonight.

"I could take Mr. Lavy in for questioning, ma'am," O'Reilly continued, "if you want to press charges."

"Absolutely not. William wasn't the problem."

The deputy nodded. "Then I'll have a look

around." He glared at Will. "Stay put until I'm done."

William felt like a kid again. "I'm not going anywhere."

More rain started to fall as O'Reilly circled the house, his flashlight illuminating the yard and the thick forest behind the house.

Julianne glanced at the dark sky. "You're getting wet, William. Climb the steps to the porch."

"I'll stay here, Jules."

"You're mad at me."

"What?" He didn't understand her comment. "Why would you say that?"

"Because I called the sheriff's office."

"Someone was at your door. I would have been frightened, too." He glanced at a distant stand of trees. "I chased him across the drive, but when he ran into the woods, I knew it was useless to follow. Plus, I was concerned about you."

She rubbed her hands together and frowned. "I don't understand why you came back tonight?"

He shrugged. "Maybe it was the storm or because I was worried about you being alone. Maybe I just wanted to make sure you were all right."

She stared at him for a long moment and then nodded. "Whatever the reason, I'm grateful, which is something I keep saying. Thank you, William."

The deputy approached the outbuildings and tugged on the doors of the various buildings. The workshop door hung open. O'Reilly stepped inside. The arc of his flashlight played over the interior of the shop. Eventually, he returned to the house.

"Someone's been rummaging around in there, Ms. Graber. Have you been in your father's shop since you returned home?"

"Only tonight. I told you, the man in the mask was waiting in the darkness for me." She rubbed her hands together. "The sheriff planned to question a vagrant about last night's attack. Do you know what happened?"

"The man had an alibi."

"So he's not in jail?"

"That's correct." O'Reilly pointed to the door. "Why don't you go inside, ma'am. I'll talk to you in a few minutes. First, I need to get a statement from Mr. Lavy."

"But I told you, he came here to check on me."

"Yes, ma'am, I heard you."

"Would you care for a cup of coffee?" she offered.

"No, ma'am, but don't let me stop you."

With a nod, Julie stepped inside and closed the door.

O'Reilly wanted information, especially why William had come back tonight to check on Julianne. What should he tell him? That he couldn't get Julianne off his mind? The truth was he'd been worried about her safety and had wanted to see her again.

The deputy had told Julianne to go inside, but as soon as she closed the door behind her, all her pent-up anxiety spilled out with a swell of tears. Refusing to give her emotions free rein, she fisted her hands, then brushed her fingers across her cheeks.

Pulling in a deep breath, she hurried to the kitchen to make coffee. Between sniffs, she threw another log into the woodstove, stoked the flames and then boiled water that she poured over the grounds in the drip coffeepot. The hearty smell of the beans filled the kitchen. She reached for a tissue, blew her nose and hurried upstairs to change into jeans and a sweater.

Lifting a small mirror from her makeup bag, she groaned at the sight of her tangled hair and splotched face. Not that she cared what the deputy thought. Or William.

Although, she didn't want to seem needy or weak. Her father had insisted both his children work hard and were able to take care of themselves. Her Aunt Mary thought Julie was too independent, yet her aunt had survived for all these years on her own as a single Amish woman.

Truth be told, living alone wasn't what Julianne wanted. Growing up, she had longed for a man to love her. Like every other Amish girl, she wanted to court and marry and raise a family. That dream had died along with Bennie and her dad.

Quickly, she changed and descended the steps just as a knock sounded at the door. She opened it and peered to where William stood near the patrol car. His gaze held hers and made a thread of concern tangle around her spine. Surely Deputy O'Reilly didn't think William would cause her harm?

The deputy stepped into view. "I'd like to ask you a few questions, ma'am."

She motioned him forward. "Certainly, come in."

He followed her into the house and handed her the coat he was holding. "I found this outside and presume it belongs to you."

"The man pulled it off of me in the scuffle." She hung her wet jacket on a wall peg and pointed to the aluminum pot on the stove.

"I brewed coffee in case you've changed your mind and you'd like a cup. Mr. Lavy could join us."

"You'll have to ask Mr. Lavy after I leave."

"You and William knew each other in your youth as I recall."

The deputy pulled out a notepad and pen. "That was a long time ago."

"Things change, right?"

"Yes, ma'am. A lot has happened since then. I knew your brother. He was a great guy. I never…"

Julianne turned away and hugged her arms. Mention of Bennie brought back too many memories. She glanced at the rag rug. It looked out of place near the stairs and seemed like a large neon light that flickered in the darkness. *Blood! Beware of the blood!*

"Did you hear me, Ms. Graber?"

She turned back and shook her head. "I'm sorry. Could you repeat your question?"

"Would you go over the sequence of events tonight? I want to record what happened."

"I told you everything when we were outside. Do I need to repeat myself?"

"Yes, ma'am, you do. I'll record your statement. Once I get back to the station, I'll type up your report and ask you to stop by the office on your next trip to town to sign the typed statement."

They sat at the kitchen table, and Julianne repeated what she had told the deputy earlier. At the conclusion of her testimony, she glanced through the window at the lights that continued to flash on the cruiser and thought back to that day long ago when the sheriff and his deputies had arrived at her house. She had stayed with William at the Lavy home until her aunt arrived and whisked her away to Willkommen.

At times, when she closed her eyes, she could still see the flashing lights and William standing at the end of the drive, his face pulled in worry as she rode away in her aunt's buggy with the cold air blowing through her hair. She shivered with the memory.

"Are you cold, ma'am?"

She rubbed her arms. "A bit, yes. I'll pour a cup of coffee to warm up." As she stood, she glanced at his phone sitting on the table. "Surely you have enough information?"

He tapped his phone and jammed it into

his pocket. "I have enough. I'll be leaving shortly. Do you plan to remain here tonight?"

"I have no place else to go."

He handed her his business card. "This has the sheriff's department phone number. Program it into your cell. I'll swing by your farm a couple more times until my shift ends. The next deputy on duty will do the same."

"With all the lights flashing, I doubt the prowler will return." A least that was her hope.

"You'll come by the office to sign your statement?" the deputy asked.

She nodded. "In a day or two."

"That works for me. I'll keep you posted in case anything develops."

"Deputy O'Reilly, let me ask you something."

"Shoot."

She didn't like his choice of words. "Were you here when my father and brother died? Did you come into my house that day?"

His face paled. "No, ma'am. I wasn't with

the department at that time. I signed on two years later."

"But you've heard talk."

His brow raised. "Talk?"

"What's the consensus around the office?"

"About the murder-suicide?"

"Has anyone questioned whether that's what happened?"

"You mean, does anyone think Bennie didn't kill your dad?"

"I guess that's what I'm asking."

"No, ma'am. The sheriff made the ruling, and everyone agrees with him one hundred percent."

"One hundred percent?" Her heart sank.

"Yes, ma'am."

He started for the door and then turned. "Thank you, ma'am, for answering my questions. Lock your doors. Call if you need anything."

She nodded. "I appreciate your thoroughness."

He let himself out. She watched from the window as he talked to William for a few minutes and then rounded his car to the driver's side.

She took her mug back to the kitchen and turned down the oil lamp. A knock sounded at the door.

Pulling it open, she expected to see William. Instead, Deputy O'Reilly stood on the porch, his gaze pensive.

"There was one person, ma'am."

She didn't understand his statement.

"One person on the force," O'Reilly continued. "An old-timer. He knew your dad. Ike Vaughn. You might remember him."

She shook her head. "I don't recognize the name."

"Ike was an easygoing guy, never stirred the pot, so to speak. He retired early, turned in his badge and moved to a cabin about twenty miles north of town."

She waited, unsure where the deputy was going.

"I ran into him not long ago when he was having a cup of coffee at the Country Kitchen. We chatted for a minute. I inquired how he was doing, you know, being neighborly."

Julianne did know.

"And…" she said, hoping the deputy would get to his point.

"Here's the thing. You asked about anyone questioning the murder-suicide decision."

Julianne's heart pounded. "Yes."

"Ike told me he disagreed with the sheriff. That's why he turned in his badge. He said the sheriff was wrong."

"About what happened?"

O'Reilly nodded. "That's right. He said Bennie wasn't a murderer, and your dad never would have become violent with his son."

"Did he say what he thought had happened?"

The deputy hesitated for a long moment. "I don't want to say anything against the sheriff, ma'am."

"Of course, I won't repeat anything you tell me."

"Ike said it wasn't a murder-suicide. He said Bennie hadn't killed himself. He said, without a shadow of a doubt, it was a double homicide."

* * *

William waved farewell as Deputy O'Reilly turned his car onto the main road and headed back to town. Once the patrol car disappeared from sight, Will glanced at Julianne's house. His clothes were wet and stuck to him, and a light rain continued to fall. As much as he longed to join Julianne in her kitchen, the door to the farmhouse remained closed.

He hurried home, chastising himself for allowing a woman to upset his peace and calm. In his youth, he had been attracted to pretty girls. Then he had noticed Julianne, and he could think of no one else. After Bennie and her father died, she had disappeared from William's life, and he had survived. In fact, he had found a renewed sense of fulfillment when he returned home to care for his father. Even after his *datt*'s passing, William had taken comfort in the daily labor that maintaining a farm required. Cultivating the soil, planting the fields and harvesting the crops, as well as tending to the livestock, had provided a balm for his formerly troubled soul.

Since Julianne had returned to Mountain Loft, his peaceful routine had been turned upside down, as if another man had taken up residence in his body—a man filled with thoughts of green eyes and auburn hair. Along with those thoughts came the memories of moonlight and a kiss.

Upon entering his kitchen, he hung his hat and waistcoat on the wall pegs near the back door, then he added a log to the woodstove and heated the last of the coffee still remaining in the pot. Mug in hand, he hurried to his bedroom and changed into dry clothes. The rain stopped, but he remained unsettled. Sipping the reheated brew, he peered down the road through the darkness, hoping to catch sight of her house in spite of the fog that had rolled in and blocked the Graber farm from view.

Although he was concerned about Julianne's safety, he wouldn't disturb her again. Footsteps on her porch might throw her into more of a tailspin, but he hoped the sound of a buggy would be less unsettling.

He slipped on a dry coat, adjusted his hat on his head and hurried to the barn to hitch his mare to the buggy. He lit two lamps and hung them on hooks above the rear wheels to alert other vehicles of his presence before he climbed onto the seat. Grabbing the reins, he encouraged Sugar forward. The clip-clop of the mare's hooves sounded in the fog as he headed to the Graber farm.

He turned into the drive and pulled Sugar to a stop near the open gate. The door to the woodshop was shut, and he again wondered why the prowler had gone there. William had seen someone on the porch peering into the house. If only he could have caught the culprit.

He thought back to the Graber murders. Julianne claimed someone had knocked her out and then left the house. Who was it, and why had he spared Julianne's life? If he had spared her life then, had he returned tonight to finish the job he had left undone nearly five years ago?

William glanced again at her house. A curtain in an upstairs window moved. Were his eyes playing tricks on him in the foggy night, or was Julianne peering at him through the glass?

He nodded his head almost imperceptibly, hoping to assure her that he meant no harm and would not disturb her as he stood guard throughout the night.

In his youth, William had been anything but trustworthy. Reputations were hard to change. If only Julianne would realize that by returning to his faith, he had become a new man, hopefully a better man, but a man who still carried the memory of that night at the lake in his heart.

SIX

Julianne woke the next morning with a start. She glanced at her phone on the nightstand, where she had left it. Nine a.m. How had she slept so late?

Feeling rested, she stretched her arms and remembered hearing the clip-clop of a horse's hooves after the deputy had returned to town. At first, she thought someone was riding by on the road, then she'd heard the buggy turn into the drive. Her heart had stopped, as she'd feared the prowler had returned, but as she peered from the window, she had recognized William.

Even with the fog, there was no mistaking the bulk of him and the way he angled his head to stare at the surrounding area. His gaze had stayed focused on her father's woodshop for some time. She had lowered the curtain, wondering what he was doing, and then minutes later, she had peered again. That time, he had seen her and had nodded.

Tears of gratitude burned her eyes. William seemed to appear whenever she was in danger, as if he could sense her need. His pensive gaze and the concern she saw in his eyes warmed a place in her heart that longed for healing. She'd been so needy since returning home, her emotions hiding just below the surface.

Crawling from bed, she approached the window and eased back the curtain. The drive was empty. William had probably left sometime this morning. Disappointment swept over her. For half a moment, she had thought about making breakfast and inviting him inside for coffee and eggs. A silly thought, especially since he was probably back at his farm.

She dressed, hurried downstairs and stepped onto her porch. The storm had brought a crispness to the air and a drop in temperature that made her shiver. She went back inside, stoked the fire and brewed half a pot of coffee.

Today, she planned to clean the upstairs. Brad Abbott would arrive by eleven, and she wanted the house to be at its best. She didn't want to sell her farm to a developer who would divide her property into small tracts of land. More than anything, she wanted the farm to remain intact and the house to go to a *gut* family.

Gut? She smiled at her Amish slip. Selling to an Amish family would mean the farm would carry on as her father and mother would have wanted.

She glanced at the small cement markers on the hill. A developer would plow the land. What would happen to the grave sites? She couldn't sell to someone who wouldn't care for the land or the graves, no matter what the real-estate agent said or how much money a buyer would be willing to pay for the farm.

By eleven o'clock, the upstairs was clean. She had changed into a skirt and sweater and had pulled her hair into a bun like she used to do in her Amish days. To get the hair out of her face had been her excuse, although she had formed the bun out of habit before giving thought to what she was doing.

Hearing the approach of a vehicle, she peered out the kitchen window and watched a white SUV pull into her drive. The windows were tinted, and she waited until the driver's door opened to be sure it was the real-estate agent.

Glancing at the Lavy farm, she hoped to catch sight of William working in the fields, but she didn't see him or his buggy in the barnyard or the surrounding pastures.

Brad climbed to the porch. After swallowing down a surge of nervous anxiety, she pulled in a deep breath and squared her shoulders before she opened the door.

"You're right on time." She motioned him inside.

He stuck out his hand and grasped hers, holding it a bit longer than she would have liked. "Good to see you again, Julianne. The place looks better than I expected."

"What did you expect?" she asked.

"Overgrown pastures and peeling paint."

She didn't mention William's care of the property. "As a real-estate agent, I thought you would have driven by the farm a number of times."

His smirk included a hint of embarrassment. "I rarely go to the lake. William Lavy's farm is the only other property out this way. I stopped at his house on the way here to see if he was interested in selling."

"Why would you think he might be?"

"From what I've heard, William didn't plan to remain within the Amish community. Sometimes an offer from a buyer is all that's needed to sway a man's heart."

"You've heard this in town?" she asked, knowing full well that his receptionist, Gloria, was more than likely his source.

"The Country Kitchen is a gathering spot for many of the townspeople. I hear talk."

He probably had heard lots of talk over the years of the murder-suicide that had rocked the small town and set tongues wagging. Julianne wondered if they were still gossiping about that terrible night.

"Did William agree to a meeting?" she asked, flicking her gaze once again to his farm. If only he would appear out of thin air, like he had last night.

"No one answered the door, and his buggy was gone. Evidently, he's not at home."

That made Julianne even more unsettled. Brad Abbott was glib and self-assured. Too self-assured.

Brad raised his brow. "You're the last house along this lane, Julianne, with only the lake beyond. I understand your desire to sell the place after everything that happened. Must be hard to stay the night when you're so isolated. Mountain Loft has had problems with prowlers recently. Be careful and on guard."

His warning sounded somewhat like a threat. "Are you trying to scare me off my property?"

"I can assure you—" He held up his hands in apology. "No such thought entered my mind. I was offering advice to a person I hope will be one of my clients."

He glanced at the stairway. "Shall we start the tour upstairs?"

She nodded and motioned for him to climb the stairs ahead of her. Brad had cautioned her to be on her guard, which was good advice. She would watch her back and keep her eye on him.

Stopping at the top of the stairs, she heard a buggy pull into the drive. She glanced outside and smiled with relief as William guided his mare toward the barn.

He had guarded her throughout the night, and now he was coming to check on her. Once again, his timing was perfect. Brad's visit had her on edge, and his comments had made her even more concerned about her safety, especially when William wasn't nearby.

"The rooms are quite spacious for an Amish home," Brad said as he met her in the hallway. "There's another bedroom downstairs?"

"That's right." She descended the stairs

and pointed to what had been the family guest room. As he entered the room, she stepped into the kitchen and opened the back door.

William pointed to the real-estate agent's car. "Looks like you've got company."

"Brad wanted to see the house."

"I'll be out here if you need me."

She smiled and returned to the main room just as Brad exited the downstairs bedroom and nodded with satisfaction.

"The house is well laid out, Julianne. The open-living concept appeals to folks from the city. The hardwoods will need to be sanded and stained, a new kitchen, indoor plumbing throughout, and heat and air, electricity." He nodded again. "The cost of renovation will offset the selling price."

"What about the land?" she asked.

"Sixty-five acres, right?"

"That's correct."

He rubbed his chin. "Non-Amish farmers would be looking for more land. Now if Lavy wanted to sell, that might draw a buyer. The logical choice is divide the land into smaller tracts for development."

"You mean individual home sites?"

He nodded. "I'd like to see this area become a destination tourist spot. Winter sports in the colder months, outdoor recreation in the warmer weather. The lake would draw fishermen and boaters. Add a water park, and folks would flock here."

She doubted the local townspeople would want an influx of tourists. "What about an Amish buyer? You mentioned advertising in *The Budget*."

"That's an option, although the Amish won't give you top dollar." He pulled a paper from the binder he was holding and handed it to her. "Here's the selling price I worked up yesterday."

She glanced at the number. "This seems low for sixty-five acres."

"Raw land is a hard sale, Julianne. It could stay on the market for years."

"This isn't raw land," she countered. "It's a farm with a house and outbuildings. My father's workshop, a barn—" Frustrated, she glanced again at the paper and sighed. "Let me think it over, Brad."

"Sure. I'll get back to you in a day or two. Or stop by the office in town. Gloria will have the papers ready to sign by tomorrow afternoon."

He started for the door and then hesitated. "I'm sorry about your dad and brother. A murder-suicide is hard to understand."

She gazed at him, her heart thumping. His comment had taken her by surprise.

"Some folks will reject a property because of the history." He offered her a sympathetic smile. "Superstition runs strong in some folks. If they think a house has bad vibes—"

He continued to stare at her, and a chill slipped down her spine.

"Bad vibes?" she asked.

"You know—" He glanced at the rug she had laid over the bloodstain. "Stories abound. Folks die, then unfortunate things happen to new buyers."

"What are you saying?"

"Bad things happen in threes. It'll be hard

enough to sell a home where two people have died. I'm just saying don't let anything else happen, or it could knock the selling price down even more."

She didn't like his inference.

He opened the kitchen door. "I'll see you in a day or two."

Stepping onto the porch, the agent spied Will and chuckled. "Were your ears burning?"

"Not in the slightest. What's on your mind, Brad?"

"I stopped by your house earlier. Combining your farm with Julianne's will bring in a buyer for sure. I could work up some figures for you."

"My farm's not for sale."

"If you change your mind..."

Will's gaze narrowed. "I won't."

This time, the agent's chuckle had a nervous ring. He glanced back at Julianne. "Thanks for showing me the house. As I mentioned, Gloria will have the papers ready when you come to town."

Julie stared after him as he climbed into

his SUV and drove off her property. She hadn't appreciated his implied threats or his reference back to her father's and brother's deaths. Was he trying to scare her into signing on with his agency?

Brad Abbott hoped to make his fortune turning a quiet farm town into a mountain resort. She doubted the townspeople in Mountain Loft would buy into his grandiose ideas, and she didn't want to help him achieve his goals. Yet she had to sell her farm.

She descended the porch steps and hurried to where Will stood. "You always appear when I need support."

He smiled, and she noted a twinkle in his eye. "Just trying to help, ma'am."

The tension that had taken hold of her when she'd been with Brad dissipated. "I saw your buggy in the drive last night," she said. "You were guarding me, and I'm grateful."

"I was worried the prowler would return." He stepped closer. Fatigue lined his eyes.

"You didn't sleep," she said, stating the

obvious. "Then you were gone most of the morning."

"I had to meet someone," he said.

In the distance, she heard horse's hooves and the creak of a buggy on the lane. Turning toward the sound, she raised her hand over her eyes to block the glare of the sun.

"It seems I have another visitor."

A woman waved, and Julianne's stomach tightened. "Oh, William. What did you do?"

"I made a phone call yesterday, Julianne. You shouldn't stay alone."

"But why—?"

"To help you."

Except he wasn't helping her. He was making her face the last person she wanted to see. A person who reminded her of her father and the loss that ate at her heart. A person who didn't understand her need to leave the Amish faith and strike out on her own.

The buggy turned into the drive and came to a stop.

"Don't you understand, William? This will only make selling the farm harder for me."

Gritting her teeth with resolve, she approached the woman in the buggy.

"What a surprise to see you again, Aunt Mary."

William had thought Julianne would be happy to see her aunt, but the scowl on her face and her sharp retort told him she was less than joyous about the reunion. He watched with some trepidation as she wrapped her arms around her waist and approached the older woman's buggy.

"It's been a long time," Julie said, staring up at her aunt.

Mary's poignant expression told Will more than he'd previously realized. From what he could deduce, the two women's parting hadn't been on the best of terms.

"William called the phone shack yesterday," Mary explained. "I got the message and called him back immediately. He said you're staying here alone."

Julianne hung her head and let out a heartfelt sigh of remorse. "I'm sorry, Aunt Mary, about the way I left you."

"I knew you were ready to be on your own, although I did not expect you to leave your faith behind."

"I—I didn't know how to tell you."

"You probably realized I would have talked you into staying with me longer and remaining within the church."

"Still, I should have discussed my plans with you."

"Your letters brought me comfort. Sometimes we write that which we would not speak. Finding our way is not always easy."

The older woman got down from the buggy and stepped toward her niece. "I did not come here to convince you to change your life. I came to offer support and—" she opened her arms wide "—and love."

Julie stood for a long moment. William saw a tear roll down her cheek.

Her aunt stepped closer. "You do not have to fear me, Julianne. I want only your happiness."

With that final promise, Julie threw herself into her aunt's embrace.

William remained silent, not wanting to

disrupt the moment. When Mary Graber had called him back yesterday, he had not realized the history between the two women. The aunt's initial hesitation over the phone had made him wonder what had transpired before Julianne had branched out on her own, although Mary had quickly agreed to stay with her niece. He had left early this morning, after ensuring Julianne was safe throughout the night, and guided Mary here along the mountain road.

Pulling out of her aunt's embrace, Julianne wiped her eyes and smiled. "Let's take your things inside. I cleaned the guest room this morning and only need to put sheets and a quilt on the bed."

"I don't mean to cause more work for you, dear. I'm here to help, not hinder."

They grabbed the various totes in the back of the buggy. "Get the boxes, William, if you do not mind." Mary pointed to two cardboard boxes. "I brought food with me—jams and canned foods, as well as some baked items."

She glanced around the farm. "If I'm here long enough, I want to plant a garden."

Julianne smiled. "I'm selling the house, and there's a grocery in town where we can purchase food."

"Of course, but fresh vegetables are so much better."

William placed the boxes on the kitchen counter. "Mary, you're welcome to anything in my garden when it starts to produce. Last year, I gave what I couldn't eat to a few families in town that don't grow their own food."

"Thank you for the offer, William."

Without being prompted, Mary scurried around the kitchen and unpacked the items she had brought.

"It looks like you're planning to stay for a long time." Julianne laughed as she helped arrange the canned goods on the shelves of the pantry.

As the women worked in the kitchen, William tended to the horses, and brought hay and feed from his own farm to the barn. Once Mary's mare, Rosie, was cared for, he hurried home with a promise to join the women for the evening meal.

After completing his day's work, William washed up and changed into a clean shirt. As he raised his hand to knock on Julianne's door, he heard the women's chatter coming from the kitchen and smiled. Two women alone would be no match for a hateful man bent on causing mayhem, but there was safety in numbers, and having Aunt Mary with her should bring Julianne comfort.

Aunt Mary seemed to have settled into her new surroundings as she and Julianne served the meal. William enjoyed the sliced ham, cold slaw and pickled beets Mary had brought from her house and appreciated being invited for dinner.

After the plates were cleared, Julianne poured coffee while Mary cut the pie. "I made this last night after talking to William," she explained as she placed a large slice on the table in front of him.

"Homemade pie is something I have not had in quite some time. *Danki.*"

After dessert, the two women tidied the

kitchen and William returned to the barn to check on Rosie. Julianne joined him there. The sun was setting, and there was a chill in the air.

"Thank you again for calling Aunt Mary. I felt guilty about leaving her, and the longer I stayed away, the harder it was to reconnect." Julie shook her head. "I should have realized my sweet aunt would not hold on to anger."

"She was eager to be with you, Jules. Remember you are her closest relative. You lost your *datt*, but she, too, grieved for her brother."

"I—I was thinking of my own sorrow and should have been more considerate of her feelings. Perhaps down deep, I was afraid of her pull to keep me on her farm."

"She's sold most of her animals and only maintains a small garden. A neighbor boy is caring for her place while she is away, so do not worry. She wanted to be with you."

"And the feeling is mutual."

Julianne's face glowed in the setting light, and his neck warmed. He needed to return home before he said something he might regret, like how pretty she looked and how much he enjoyed spending time with her.

"I'll check the outbuildings before I leave. The woodshop is closed up. Remember to lock your doors. Keep your phone close at hand. I stopped at the sheriff's office when I passed through town this morning. He and his men will patrol this area and the lake more frequently, but you still need to be careful."

"I'm aware of the danger." She stretched out her hand as if to shake his, but he grabbed hold of it and stepped closer.

Staring into her green eyes, he realized how concerned he was about her safety. "Be vigilant, Julie. I don't want to scare you, but the culprit is still on the loose. Whether he's a vagrant or someone else, you need to remain alert. I don't want anything to happen to you."

He squeezed her hand and then headed to his farm. At the road, he glanced back, but Julie was already inside. The door was closed, hopefully locked, and the curtains were drawn.

Keep her safe, Gott.

As he hurried to his farm, he felt more confused than ever and was still worried about her safety. Storms rolled in throughout the night. Between the pouring rain, the lightning and thunder, he slept fitfully and rose a number of times to stare from his window at her house in the distance. Each time he did, he prayed for her again.

SEVEN

Julianne tossed and turned most of the night due to the storms, and she finally gave up trying to get any rest. Needing caffeine, she rose before dawn to stoke the woodstove in the kitchen and brew coffee before Mary got up.

After slipping into her robe and slippers, she quietly passed the guest room, hurried downstairs and stopped at the table to strike a match and light the oil lamp.

A floorboard creaked behind her.

Her neck tingled with apprehension. Still holding the ignited match, she turned toward the sound and stared into the darkness.

A hand grabbed her shoulder. She gasped, dropped the match to the floor and thrashed her arms.

How had he gotten inside?

She jabbed her elbow into his ribs. He groaned. She clawed at his hands and stomped on his instep.

He wrapped his hands around her neck. She wedged her fingers under his to keep him from cutting off her air supply and kicked her foot back. She hit his shin and kicked him again. He slapped her exactly where she had been hurt the first night.

Pain shot through her. He threw her to the floor and ran from the house.

She moaned as she crawled to her feet and stumbled to the door that was open. Her heart pounded nearly out of her chest, and her breath came in short gasps as she stared into the darkness, seeing no one.

With trembling hands, she started to close the door.

"Are you all right?" It was William's voice. He was racing along the drive. "I saw a man run into the woods behind your house."

"Oh, Will. I… I'm scared."

He hurried up the stairs, crossed the porch and wrapped her in his arms. "Let's get you inside in case he's still in the area."

She felt secure in his embrace, and together they dashed into the kitchen. The moment William released his hold on her, her fear returned, and her pulse raced from the shock of what had happened.

William closed the door, engaged the lock and jammed the top of a kitchen chair under the knob. He did the same at the front door before returning to her. With his arm protectively around her waist, he ushered her to the table, where he struck a match and lit the lamp.

Standing side by side, they looked around the house. Julianne moaned at the chaos and clutched his hand for support.

Upstairs, a door opened and closed, then footsteps sounded on the stairs. She glanced up to see Aunt Mary on the landing.

"Oh, Julianne!" Her aunt's cry tore at her heart. "Are you all right?"

She nodded, unable to find her voice.

"Someone broke in," William explained. "From the havoc, he appeared to be searching for something."

Mary raced down the stairway, nearly

tripping over her feet. She hugged Julie and rubbed her hand over William's shoulder. When she pulled back and raised her hands to her throat, her eyes were wide and her face contorted. "The house—"

Julianne looked around at the main room. Surrounded by the full magnitude of the upheaval, she rested her head on William's strong shoulder and tried to comprehend what had happened. The drawers were pulled from the cabinets, and papers from her father's desk were strewn everywhere. Tablecloths had been pulled from the chest and cluttered the floor.

Just as in the main room, the cabinets and drawers in the kitchen hung open, and items had been moved and rearranged. Even the pantry was in disarray.

Before going to bed last night, she had checked the doors and ensured they were locked. If the doors were locked, then the person who had entered the house had a key.

She shivered, knowing someone had been here while she and her aunt slept upstairs. With the raging storms, she doubted they would have heard him if he had climbed the stairs. The thought of what could have happened made her stomach roil and her heart pound even harder.

"You need to call the sheriff," William prompted her.

She stepped out of his embrace, feeling an instant chill, and fumbled to retrieve the cell she had placed in the pocket of her bathrobe earlier.

"The sheriff will wish I never returned to Mountain Loft when I tell him someone entered my house. I can't be one hundred percent sure, but the man who broke in seemed different from the man with the bandana."

"You think he was a different person?"

She nodded. "That's what worries me even more than three attacks in as many days. I didn't see a bandana."

"So at least two different people have come after you?"

Julianne feared what William said was true.

William waited on the porch after Julianne called the sheriff's office. Hearing a siren in the distance, he hurried to the end of the drive and flagged down the sheriff. "Thanks for getting here so quickly."

Sheriff Paul Taylor leaned through his open window. "Dispatch said someone entered the Graber home?"

"Julianne and her aunt are upstairs changing. I told them not to disturb the main floor. Julie surprised the burglar. He choked her, but she fought back, and he fled. The kitchen door was open, and she's sure she locked it last night."

The sheriff parked in the drive and walked to the house. He snapped a few photos of the porch, then pushed open the door and stepped inside.

He let out a breath. "It's a wonder the women didn't hear the commotion."

"It stormed all night. The thunder and the rain on the tin roof probably drowned out any noise he made."

Using his cell phone, the sheriff photographed the room from various angles. He zoomed in on a number of the papers strewn across the floor. "These look like farm documents."

"Julianne will know about them." William glanced up to see her standing on the landing.

"I came downstairs this morning to stoke the fire and brew coffee," Julianne quickly explained as she joined the men in the living area. "When I tried to light the oil lamp, he attacked me."

"The doors were locked?" the sheriff asked.

"I remember checking them last night. Mary did, as well. Yes, both entrances were locked."

"Who else has a key?"

Mary followed Julianne downstairs. "No one that either of us know about."

The sheriff shook his head in frustration, then he glared at Julianne as if she was the suspect. "Are you keeping any secrets from me, Ms. Graber? You hiding something here in the house?"

From her expression, it was clear she didn't appreciate the sheriff's comment. "I have no idea what you're talking about, nor do I know why anyone would break into the house."

"Ma'am, I hate to tell you, but you may have more than one person interested in your property. If the attacker had a key on the first and second nights, wouldn't he have entered the house those nights, as well?"

"I—I don't know, but I don't like thinking more than one person is prowling around here."

"Did you see his bandana?"

She shook her head. "It was dark this morning, but I don't recall him wearing a mask."

"Then you saw his face."

"I told you it was dark."

A second patrol car turned into the drive. The sheriff went outside to talk to the deputy, who took fingerprints and more photographs. Once the sheriff gave Aunt Mary the go-ahead to tidy the house, William helped her return the items to the various drawers and cabinets while the sheriff talked to Julianne on the porch. She frowned during most of the conversation and glanced occasionally through the window at William.

"Julianne plans to stay here until she sells the farm." Aunt Mary shook her head in frustration. "I tried to convince her to come to my house in Willkommen, but she won't hear of it."

"You could both stay at my house," he suggested.

"You're generous, but we couldn't do that."

"Of course you could, if Julianne weren't so stubborn."

Mary smiled. "She gets that from her father."

"If you won't stay with me, then I'll need to shore up your security. I saw some deadbolt locks in the workshop. I'll install them on both doors so that even with a key, the burglar won't be able to get in."

Will hurried to the workshop and came back with the locks. He drilled holes and screwed the locks in place. By the time Julianne entered the house, William had new locks on the front door and was ready to tackle the kitchen entrance.

"The sheriff is taking another look around outside." She glanced at the hardware in his hand. "Seems you've solved one of our problems."

"Stay at my house, Julianne."

"Aunt Mary and I will be fine. I'm not worried, Will."

But he knew she was. He could see it in her tired eyes and the pull on her lips.

The sheriff knocked on the door and then opened it without being invited in. "My deputy and I are heading back to town. I'll let you know if we discover anything else. We'll run those prints." He glanced at Julianne. "I don't need to tell you to keep your doors locked."

"William's installing additional locks," she said.

"They'll be a deterrent. Stay inside at night and remember trouble can strike in the daytime, as well. Is your phone charged?"

"It is, and I can charge it from my car when the battery runs down."

"That'll work. Call me if you uncover anything as you tidy up the house."

"Thank you, Sheriff."

"Did I mention there's a motel on the mountain road and a new B and B—"

"I'm staying here," she insisted.

The sheriff glanced at William. His gaze held a hint of question. "Don't forget to stop by my office, Will. I need your prints, especially since you always appear after something happens."

William had enjoyed dinner with Julianne and her aunt the night prior, which meant his fingerprints could be anywhere. Once the sheriff had his prints on file, William might go from being a helpful neighbor to a person of interest—a person of interest suspected of breaking into Julianne Graber's house.

Julianne's body ached as she lay on her bed and tried to rest after the sheriff left. She had a pounding headache. No wonder. Someone had come after her for the last three nights, and she'd been physically attacked.

The man who had broken into the house had been taller and bulkier than the man who had accosted her the first night, and his breath had a distinctive odor she couldn't identify. He had been searching for something. She'd startled him, and he had attacked her in order to get away.

What had she heard when she stared after him through the open doorway? Nothing, not the clip-clop of horses' hooves or the hum of a car engine. Had he fled her house on foot?

Even though Julianne was tired, sleep eluded her. An hour later, she hurried back downstairs to find William in the kitchen drinking coffee.

He glanced up as she entered and hesitated as if waiting for her acceptance of his presence. "Your aunt invited me to stay, but I can go if you would feel more comfortable without me."

His eyes gave him away. She saw into the depths of his goodness and his willingness to help her. She thought back to the lake and the sweetness of his kiss. If only she could change the horrific crime that had happened later that night. With a sigh, she pushed aside the memory, needing to focus on her present problem.

"A lot has taken place since I arrived home, William, and you've been with me through much of it. Bennie loved you like a brother. He could read a person's heart. I like to think that I can, as well. You've always tried to protect me."

"I'm not sure the sheriff shares that belief."

"The sheriff was mistaken about what happened to Bennie and my father. He is mistaken about you, as well."

"Julianne, I..." He reached for her hand.

The warmth of his touch buoyed her spirits. She stepped closer and looked up at him expectantly.

Aunt Mary's footsteps sounded on the stairs. "I'll have food ready in a minute," she said as she hurried to the stove, seemingly unaware of the close moment she had interrupted.

Julianne's cheeks burned.

William squeezed her hand before she

pulled away. "How about a cup of coffee?" he asked.

"That sounds *wunderbaar.*" Julianne needed coffee to get her mind off the strength of William's hold on her heart. She also needed to tell both her aunt and William about the cash supposedly hidden at the house. Was that what the prowler had been searching for last night? An even more important question was where had he gotten the key?

EIGHT

William enjoyed the late breakfast and was grateful to share the meal with Julianne and her aunt, especially after the sheriff's visit and the comment he had made about William appearing whenever Julianne was in danger. Not that the sheriff had called him a person of interest, per se, but the innuendo was there. No doubt, Julianne and her aunt were well aware of the point the sheriff had been trying to make.

When they finished eating, Aunt Mary refilled his coffee cup and then patted his hand when Julianne excused herself to get something from upstairs. "I must ask your forgiveness, William, for my comments when you wanted to talk to Julianne so long ago."

"The day I stopped by your house in Willkommen?"

Mary nodded. "I was worried. Julianne had suffered such shock. I knew you were a friend of Bennie's. The sheriff had mentioned at the beginning of his investigation that he wondered if you were involved."

"He's always held me in low esteem, which I probably deserved in my youth."

She offered him a weak smile. "When you stopped by the house that day, I was not ready to see Julianne hurt again. You were leaving home, you told me. I do not know if you remember, but you wore *Englischer* clothing, and you were driving a friend's car. I saw your desire to leave the faith reflected in your gaze, and that was not what I wanted Julianne to see, especially when she was struggling with *Gott*."

Mary glanced at the stairwell as if to ensure Julianne could not overhear their conversation. "I believe she still struggles. All of those concerns played into my decision."

William appreciated her forthrightness.

"Julianne thinks her new life is better than the plain way," Mary admitted. "I know it is the hurt she endures and the loss of her *datt* and brother. Grief weighs heavy on her heart still. She sees the world through that grief, which clouds her vision. What troubles me most is that she has turned her back on *Gott*." Mary narrowed her eyes. "Suppose she never opens her heart to the Lord? What will happen to her?"

"*Gott* forgives, Mary."

"*Yah*, but we must ask for forgiveness first. This, I believe, she does not ask." She hesitated for a moment and then squeezed William's hand. "You are a *gut* influence, and I am grateful you contacted me. Being with Julianne again fills me with hope. She would not have reached out to me on her own, so I am glad you brought us together."

Julianne hurried down the stairs and into the kitchen with an envelope in her hand. She glanced at both of them. "Is something wrong?"

"No, dear." Aunt Mary pointed to the envelope. "Is this what you wanted to show us?"

"My father wrote this note to my mother. I found it tucked away in his desk. When

I saw the papers scattered over the floor, I wondered if the burglar was searching for what was mentioned in this note."

"You have me interested." Aunt Mary moved closer as Julianne read what her father had written.

"Daniel encouraged me to handle my money wisely," Mary acknowledged when Julie was finished reading. "He said the bank was a safe institution. He also talked about investments that would grow my money."

"What type of investments?" Julianne asked.

"Mainly mutual funds and certificates of deposit. I did as he suggested through my own bank and receive a bit of interest each year, so his advice was appreciated." Mary glanced at the letter. "But I know nothing about hidden money here at the house."

"Perhaps that's why the prowler broke in," Julianne said. "Although how would he know about the secret funds?"

"Did you mention the note to the sheriff?" Mary asked.

Julianne shook her head. "I didn't mention it. He..." She glanced away.

Aunt Mary rubbed her arm. "The sheriff has a gruff manner, dear, but he means well."

"Deputy O'Reilly said someone formerly in the sheriff's department disagreed with the sheriff's determination."

"Did you get his name?" Will asked.

"Ike Vaughn. He lives higher up on the mountain. If I could get directions to his house, I'd like to talk to him."

William held up his hand. "Whoa, Julie. We've got a more immediate problem."

"You mean the man or men who keep coming after me?"

"Exactly. You and Mary should stay with me. As I mentioned, you can have the entire upstairs portion of the house. After my father's death, I moved to the spare room on the first floor."

She hesitated for a long moment. "We'll be fine here," she finally said.

"You're not thinking clearly."

"This is my family home, William. It's

my responsibility to find a good buyer for the property."

"But you don't have to stay here, Jules."

She grabbed her coffee cup and placed it in the sink, as if cutting him off. "Right now, I need to search the house for the money my father hid. If the burglar found the money, he would be long gone. He must have been searching when I startled him."

She returned to the table and stacked the plates. "I don't doubt that my *datt* would salt away money so my mother would have funds if he died. I'm just not sure where he would hide the cash."

"This is like a game of hide-and-seek, like the children play," Mary said as she helped clear the table. "Although it's much more dangerous."

After the kitchen was tidy, the three of them started at one end of the downstairs and searched every place that could be a hiding spot. William felt the floorboards, looking for a false bottom. He tapped along the walls, listening for a hollow sound. Mary and Julianne pulled open every drawer and cabinet just as the prowler had done, but ended up with nothing to show for their efforts.

"Should we look upstairs?" Aunt Mary asked.

They found nothing in the bedrooms, so they searched the outside structures, including her father's workshop and the barn, but came up empty-handed.

"The letter was written before your mother's death," William mused as they returned to the house. "It could have referred to money your father had saved long ago. Perhaps a need arose, and he used the cash."

He turned to Julianne. "Do you remember an unexpected purchase or a large payment that was due? Did your father buy more land or farm equipment? He could even have spent it at the cattle auction."

"Dad didn't discuss farm business with me. Bennie might have known, but I stayed with my mother. I can tell you the approximate amount she spent on groceries each month, but I know nothing about farm expenses, except..." She hesitated.

William watched as she chewed her lip and stared into the distance.

"Except what?" he prompted.

"Except the ledgers I reviewed yesterday showed that the farm had prospered, yet the bank account statements following his death did not reflect that properly."

"Farmers have their wealth in land and in their livestock, not necessarily as a lump sum of cash in a bank account."

"I understand what you're saying, but I don't recall any large purchases or anything out of the ordinary that would drain money from his account or make him spend the small nest egg he had secreted away for his family."

"It's a conundrum," Aunt Mary said.

"Whenever I need to ponder a situation, I think better with food in my stomach. Plus, it is well into the afternoon. Let's have some cold cuts and cheese and finish the meal with a cup of coffee and a slice of pie." She looked at William. "Does that sound *gut*?"

"It sounds perfect," he said as they hurried inside.

The cold cuts were filling, and the coffee and pie boosted their spirits as they discussed various reasons the money might no longer be on the property. By the time they finished dessert, they were as confused as they had been earlier about the funds.

"You should stay with me to ensure your total safety," William said again as he helped the women with the dishes. "You will sleep more soundly and will not have to worry about strange sounds you hear in the night."

"I understand and appreciate your concern," Julianne assured him, "but we'll be fine."

He wasn't sure of any such thing. "I have chores to do and animals to feed. If you change your mind, know that the offer remains."

He left mildly frustrated that Julianne insisted upon remaining at home. Dark clouds stretched across the horizon, and he feared more storms would pass through in the night. Whether a prowler appeared at her door or not, the storms would disturb her slumber.

His own sleep would be unsettled as he worried about what could be happening at her house. William was confident the locks would hold the doors and keep anyone from entering using a key, but windows could be broken, and sly foxes had ways of sniffing out their prey.

Julianne thought she could confront her assailant, but she hadn't been able to cock her father's rifle, and she'd trembled when the police had arrived. For all her bravado, she was scared, and for good reason.

Maybe Aunt Mary would talk some sense into Julianne as night fell. He would prepare two guest rooms, just in case. If only the women would realize they were safe with him.

Or was that the problem? Did Julianne still question whether he had changed his life for the better? She could trust him. He knew that for sure, but did she?

The house had seemed full earlier in the day when William was with them, but as night fell and the storm clouds rolled overhead, the house turned dark and cold. Julie lit the oil lamps and added a log to the woodstove.

Aunt Mary fixed an egg omelet with ham and sliced bread for dinner. Julie declined another piece of pie and felt overcome with fatigue after the dishes were washed and dried.

"You look tired," Aunt Mary said as they returned the last of the dishes to the cupboard.

"I haven't slept much since I arrived." She glanced through the window at the trees bending in the wind. "If the storm hits, I may not sleep much tonight."

"We could stay with William," Mary suggested.

Julianne nodded. "We could, although I hate to be a burden."

Mary smiled knowingly. "I doubt you could be that, but think about accepting his offer. It might be safer."

"I'll talk to William in the morning," Julianne said. "But I'm tired tonight and need to get to bed."

"I'll follow you upstairs, dear, as soon as I finish my coffee."

Julianne prepared for bed and then peered from the upstairs window, seeing the Lavy farm in the distance. A light in the kitchen window filled her with a sense of comfort, as if knowing William was nearby added a layer of protection.

She thought again of the locks he had installed, appreciating his resourcefulness. Even if the burglar returned with a key, she and Aunt Mary would be safe. At least, for tonight. Tomorrow, after a good night's sleep, she would be able to think more clearly about accepting William's offer.

She heard Mary's footsteps coming up the stairs and hurried to open her bedroom door. "I'm glad you're here, Aunt Mary. Thank you!"

"Of course, dear. I wouldn't want you to be alone. The two years you were with me brought joy to my heart. I am relieved we can be together again."

"I... I'm sorry."

"For leaving? Do not fret. You needed to

gain your independence. I understood completely, even if I didn't want you to leave." She stretched out her hand and touched Julianne's cheek. "We're family. That means we want the best for each other. My heart broke from the pain I saw in your eyes for so long after Bennie and Daniel died. For some time, I did not know if you would be able to heal."

"Without your love, I wouldn't have."

"It was not my love, dear, it was your own determination and will to survive. And *Gott*, Who did not want more pain to come into your life. You can turn to Him."

Julie shook her head. "I don't think He would listen to a woman who is not sure of His love."

"You can question, Julie. I will pray that your questions draw you back to your faith. Life is easier and richer with *Gott*, but it is your choice. I will not stand in your way, although I will continue to pray for you."

She patted Julie's arm and then moved to the guest room.

Uplifted by Aunt Mary's love, Julie slipped

into bed and closed her eyes, but before she fell asleep, a clap of thunder shattered her sense of calm. She hurried to the window and stared into the gathering storm. In the distance, she saw something move.

A man rounded the corner of the barn and stared at the house.

She stepped away from the window, her mouth dry and her ears ringing. The prowler had return. Or was it her attacker? Or the burglar?

He was dressed in black and wore a red bandana over his face. Her heart nearly stopped beating, and fear tangled around her spine.

She reached for her cell phone. No bars. No service. Probably due to the storm.

Her hands trembled and a lump of anxiety lodged in her throat.

Why hadn't she accepted William's offer to stay at his house? She would have been safe with him, but she'd needed to prove to herself that she was strong. Was it because the sheriff claimed Bennie had killed their dad? A murder-suicide placed a huge mark on her family. Was she trying to redeem her family name?

More than anything, she wanted to be with William now. He would keep her safe, she knew that for sure, but she had rejected his invitation. Because of her stubborn determination to sell her father's farm, she could lose more than a night's sleep. She could also lose her life.

Too many cups of coffee coupled with his worry about Julianne's and her aunt's safety kept William up late into the night. Or maybe it was the howling wind and torrential rain that had him on edge. The storm kept coming and mimicked his own inner storm. After stoking his wood-burning stove, he settled into his bent-hickory rocker and reached for his Bible, the small leather-bound volume that had belonged to his grandmother. She had passed during his teen years, and her dying wish was for William to remain in the faith. With gnarled fingers, she had placed her Bible in his hands. Her murky eyes had cleared for a long moment as she stared at him with love. He remembered the warmth that had settled over him during that moment, knowing his grandmother saw beyond his disruptive actions and the mistakes he made and instead focused on his goodness.

He had accepted the Bible from her, thinking he would leave it unread, but upon his return home to care for his father, the worn pages had soothed his troubled soul. As he read of God's forgiveness, he was filled with a desire to embrace his father even more. When he'd finally found the courage to ask forgiveness from both his Heavenly Father and his earthly *datt*, William had seen his own past in a new light. No longer focusing on his mistakes, he was able to see a youth who was searching for love and affirmation. He had received both from *Gott* and then eventually from his father before his death.

He wished the same for Julianne. She was running from her past and from the hurt of her father's and brother's deaths. In some way, she felt what had happened was her fault. That burden had made her flee from everything she had been raised to believe. Whether she would ever return to the Lord, William did not know. If only she would turn back to her Amish upbringing, she might find what she was searching for— namely forgiveness and affirmation.

The storm grew in strength, and he peered from the kitchen window. The Graber house sat dark in the night, and was almost impossible to see through the pouring rain. Surely, no prowler would be afoot tonight. Everyone, even the most hardened criminal, would be hunkered down at home. At least, that's what William kept telling himself.

Knowing he needed sleep, even if his mind kept swirling with thoughts of Julianne, he placed the Bible on the side table and extinguished the oil lamp.

A crash of thunder rocked the house. The strike had been close. Knowing how lightning could split a tree in two, he thought of the tall oak trees near Julianne's house and the branches that might fall on the farmhouse. Death could come in so many unforeseen ways.

He shut the thought from his mind and started for the bedroom.

A car pulled into his drive. A rush of footsteps sounded on the porch. His heart pounded with worry about what could be wrong. There was a knock at the door. Then another and another.

"William?" Julianne's plaintive voice came from outside.

He threw open the door. "Are you all right?"

She stood on his doorstep, her hair wet, her eyes wide and confusion in her gaze.

Aunt Mary climbed the steps more slowly.

"What's wrong?" he asked.

"The man in the bandana came back," Julie said. "He hovered around outside and then disappeared. I was wrong about remaining at my house. We can't stay there alone, William. Mary and I need your help."

He opened his arms and pulled her inside, feeling the beating of her heart and the softness of her embrace. Mary remained on the porch, shaking her head and staring into the darkness.

"Hurry, Mary." William motioned the older woman into the house and locked the door behind her.

"Who's doing this, William?" Julianne dropped her head into her hands. "Someone wants me to leave my property. I don't know why, but I need to find out who it is and why he wants to do me harm. I…"

She looked up at him. Her eyes glistened with tears. "I need your help. I can't do it alone. My phone wouldn't work tonight due to the storm. Tomorrow, I'm going to town to talk to the sheriff. A hateful man is on the loose, maybe two. I need protection."

William drew her closer. "You're here now. I'll keep you safe."

She rested her head on his shoulder and started to cry. Her tears broke his heart. He shouldn't have left her tonight, no matter how determined she had been to stay at her own house. Julianne needed to realize she didn't have to do everything on her own. William wanted to help her and protect her and keep her safe.

If only she would let him.

He also wanted to tell her about the feelings that swirled within him and made him want to wrap her even more tightly in his embrace, but this wasn't the time or place. Tonight, he needed to be William, the neighbor, who would give her shelter, instead of the man who remembered their long-ago kiss on a moonlit night.

NINE

Julianne hurried downstairs the next morning to find Aunt Mary at the kitchen stove. Warm biscuits sat in a basket on the table.

"I overslept," she apologized. "How can I help you?"

"You needed to sleep. William is outside. Call him for breakfast. I'm sure he is hungry."

"You waited for me?"

"Of course, dear." Aunt Mary smiled. "Although had you slept much longer, I would have awakened you. My stomach was getting hungry as well."

"I'm embarrassed."

"*Ack*, this is not necessary. You have not rested because of the danger hovering outside your house since you arrived home. Finally, you felt secure when we came to William's house."

"I should have agreed to come here earlier, Aunt Mary. You were right."

"You had to arrive at that decision in your own time. Now call William while I fry the eggs."

William was pouring feed into one of the troughs when Julianne hurried outside and waved to get his attention. "Breakfast will be on the table by the time you wash up at the water pump."

"Tell Aunt Mary I will enjoy her cooking." He finished filling the feed trough and then hurried to where Julianne stood. "You look more rested this morning."

His smile caused her cheeks to warm. She appreciated the openness of his gaze and the lightness of his tone. "Evidently, I needed sleep."

"Sleep is fitful when we are worried about what might happen. Storms are unsettling, and having someone out to do us harm is even more so. I'm glad you decided to stay here. The room was comfortable?"

She nodded. "Thank you for preparing it

for me. The quilt was beautiful. I presume your mother made it?"

"Along with her mother, my *mammi*, before my *mamm* married. It covered my bed when I was a boy."

"Such a lovely heirloom. Perhaps I should not use it."

"It is to be used and enjoyed. I am glad you could get the sleep you needed."

"You're probably behind on your chores after all you've done for me, but..." She hesitated, unsure how to ask him. "If you have time, I would appreciate your company when I talk to the sheriff in town."

"The morning chores are done. Anything else can wait. Of course, I will go with you. Aunt Mary can join us, or if she chooses to remain here, she will be safer than if she were at your house."

When they went inside, Mary declined their offer. "William has a stocked pantry and a good supply of flour and canned fruit. I will enjoy baking while you are gone. Do not worry about me. The man in the bandana is interested in you, Julianne. He will not look for an older Amish woman on a neighboring farm."

"We will go only if you promise to lock the doors and stay inside," Julianne said.

"*Yah*, I will be busy in the kitchen until your return."

"Do you need anything from the grocery store?"

Aunt Mary's eyes brightened. "A few items. I will write a shopping list, but only if you have time."

"We will make time," William said. "Besides, right now I want to check Julie's house and make sure nothing was harmed either by the storm or the prowler."

After clearing the table and washing the breakfast dishes, Julianne tucked the list Aunt Mary had given her in her purse and met William outside.

"Was everything okay at my house?" she asked.

"A few broken twigs littered the drive, but the outbuildings and house were secure. I brought back your aunt's mare and buggy. Both are in the barn."

"Thank you, William."

"Watch out for each other," Mary called to them as they climbed into Julianne's car.

"Don't forget to lock the door." Julianne waved goodbye. Once on the road, she turned to William sitting next to her in the passenger seat. "Reassure me Aunt Mary will be safe."

"I'm not worried about your aunt, Julianne, but I am worried about you."

She shrugged off his concern. "You're with me, William, so there's nothing to fear."

The morning was overcast, but the storms had ended, and after a good night's sleep, Julianne had a new perspective on the day. Being with William brought comfort and a sense of security.

"Thanks again for coming with me." She glanced at William's long legs and muscular arms and chest.

He caught her gaze, causing her cheeks to burn.

She smiled back at him for a moment too long. In that split second, a white SUV pulled out of an intersecting farm road in front of them.

Julianne slammed on the brakes. Her car skidded across the still-damp road, missing a collision with the other vehicle by no more than a hair. She gasped, clutched the wheel and worked to get her Honda back in the right-hand lane as the SUV accelerated.

"Where'd that car come from?" Julianne's pulse raced.

"The road leads to an abandoned farmhouse not far from the old quarry." William stared in the direction from which the car had come. "No telling why anyone would be back there."

"He didn't even slow down."

"If you hadn't hit the brakes, we would have rear-ended him. Good work, Jules."

"Did you get the license-plate number?" she asked.

Will shook his head. "It was smeared with mud."

"Brad Abbott drives an SUV, and he's interested in abandoned property. Plus, the man who chased me the night I arrived home drove a white car."

"An SUV?"

"I couldn't tell."

"We'll mention it to the sheriff."

But the sheriff wasn't in his office when they arrived in town. Deputy O'Reilly had left Julianne's typed statement at the reception desk. She read and signed the form as a rather young deputy took William's fingerprints. Once the task was completed, she returned the signed statement to the deputy and then explained about the white SUV that had nearly caused an accident.

"The sheriff needs to know," Julianne insisted. "Will he be back later today?"

"At some point. He's in a meeting with the mayor. I'll tell him you were here."

"Let him also know someone was prowling around my house again."

"The sheriff said you'd had problems."

Julianne titled her head and eyed the youthful deputy. "What kind of problems?"

"Only that your farm will be hard to sell. Word travels, and folks don't want to buy a house where something tragic happened." He shrugged. "You know what he meant— the murder-suicide case."

"It sounds as if the sheriff is spreading rumors."

"Not rumors, ma'am. He's just telling the truth."

"The truth is, Deputy, someone has trespassed on my property a number of times, he's attacked me and he's broken into my home. The man—or men—need to be apprehended."

"Yes, ma'am. I'll tell the sheriff."

The deputy's comments tore a hole in her heart, and a number of holes were there already. Her brother wasn't a murderer, no matter what the sheriff claimed.

"Don't pay attention to the deputy," William said once they were outside.

"He was parroting his superior officer, which only confirms my earlier upset with Sheriff Taylor. In my opinion, it's time for him to retire."

"He's up for reelection this fall." She saw

the twinkle in William's eyes. "If you're still in town, you can campaign against him."

"That's a good reason to stay in Mountain Loft," she said with a smile.

A tingle of heat crawled along her neck as he continued to hold her gaze. She wanted to spend more time with William, but he was Amish and she had left the faith. Any attraction between them needed to be quelled.

"We'll come back later, but let's stop by the real-estate office," she said, hoping to turn her focus back to the problem at hand. "I want to check up on Brad Abbott."

Gloria was sitting behind her desk when they entered. The immediate blush to the woman's cheeks and the interest in her eyes as she gazed at William was hard to miss, and it told Julianne everything she had suspected.

"Brad's been in a meeting with the mayor all morning," she told Julianne, although her attention remained focused on William.

"Are you sure he wasn't visiting an abandoned farmhouse near the old quarry?"

"I'm sure. He stopped in here bright and

early before he headed to the mayor's office."

"Does the mayor meet with everyone in town?"

Gloria pulled her gaze away from William long enough to nod at Julianne. "The mayor meets with a few business leaders, the president of the bank and the sheriff almost weekly to talk about the direction the town's going in."

"What direction would that be?" Julie asked.

Gloria offered her a quizzical stare. "The town expansion. It's this year's focus. People moving to town is good for business and brings needed revenue. A task force was convened a few months ago to encourage growth."

"Having more folks buying homes will be good for Brad's real-estate business," Julianne stated.

The receptionist nodded. "And other businesses in town, as well."

"Brad's coordinating with a developer from Atlanta?" Julianne threw out a line, like the fishermen at the lake, and wondered what she would catch.

"McDonough Homes. Ted McDonough will be in town tomorrow."

"To look at possible home sites?" Julianne asked.

"Brad must have talked to you about the project?"

He hadn't talked to her. In fact, he had led her to believe folks from Atlanta would not be interested in moving to Mountain Loft.

"I'll let Brad know you were here," Gloria said as they turned to leave.

Julianne was more convinced than ever that listing her property with Abbott Real Estate was a bad idea. She wanted her farm sold intact, instead of dividing the land into multiple home sites.

"Let's stop at Jones Grocery and pick up the items Aunt Mary requested," Julianne said as they climbed into her car.

The grocer was equally as welcoming as he had been on her first visit to his store. "How's the sale of your property going?" Harvey asked as Julianne began to gather items into a shopping basket. "Brad Abbott said he was out there yesterday."

"He was, but I may list the property myself. Do you have any For Sale by Owner signs that I could post on my drive?"

"At the end of the next aisle. I don't want to talk out of turn, but I think you're making a mistake, Julianne. Brad has connections."

In spite of Brad's connections, she didn't want her property turned into a subdivision of prefabricated homes. "He was in a meeting with the mayor when Will and I stopped by his office. Something about town expansion."

Harvey nodded. "That's the mayor's top priority. I have to admit, it won't hurt my business, either."

"But do you want city folks streaming to town?"

"Only if they're good people who plan to keep Mountain Loft as it is today. You know my ancestors worked hard to maintain the town after the gold rush ended in Georgia." He looked at the plaque on the wall with pride, as if recalling the history passed down through his family. "When the miners seeking their fortunes headed to California, my family's written history that's been passed down to me mentioned hard times and slow growth. Eventually the town became viable again. I don't want to see it decline."

"Which is doubtful," William said. "The mountains are always a draw and attract people from all over the state."

"Dahlonega has grown faster than the locals expected," Julianne added. "The college brings in folks, and Atlanta continues to spread north with communities that butt up almost to Dahlonega. It's only a matter of time until folks discover the beauty of Mountain Loft."

"You know about the dome of the main building on the Dahlonega campus is covered with gold from the Georgia mines," Harvey said with pride. He took pleasure in the fact that his family had founded Mountain Loft and that his store had been in business since the 1800s.

She nodded. "That's part of the information I share with tourists who stop in the shop where I work. Georgia gold covers the dome of the state capitol, as well."

"Some folks believe there's more gold in the hills, although it seems doubtful." Harvey smiled. "We all know, the best gold is money earned from hard work and then banked or invested."

"Fool's gold is just that," William said. "The idea of striking it rich in the abandoned mines or panning in the creeks and streams is for fools, I fear."

Julianne appreciated the conversation and the opportunity to visit with Harvey Jones. Seeing him warmed her heart and brought good memories of better days to mind. "Tell Nancy hello," she said after they purchased the groceries.

As William loaded the bags into her car, Julianne noticed an Amish woman crossing the street and heading in their direction.

Her heart lurched. "Emma?"

Surprise wrapped around the other woman's slender face. "Oh, Julianne, you are a sight to behold. I heard you had come home."

Emma smiled a greeting to William and then clutched Julie's hand. "You've come home to live?"

"To sell my farm. William and I ran in to your husband at the Country Kitchen the day after I arrived."

A pink blush spread over Emma's cheeks. She was obviously pregnant and rested her hand on her rounded stomach. "Mose and I married three years ago." She smiled apologetically. "I never thought I would marry after..."

Tears filled her eyes. She glanced away.

Julianne squeezed her hand. "Of course, you would find someone else. Bennie would have wanted you to be happy."

Although Emma looked anything but happy.

William stood to the side, giving them a chance to talk privately, which Julianne appreciated.

"Mose is a decent man," Emma said as if defending her husband. Again her hand rubbed against her protruding abdomen.

"When is the baby due?"

"Two months from now."

Seeing Emma's upset, Julianne wanted to draw her friend back to a topic that was current, and not what could have been if Bennie was still alive. "You're living with Mose's family?" Julie asked, even though she knew the answer.

"Until we can find a place of our own." Emma's voice dropped to little more than a whisper. "People talk, as you have probably heard. It still breaks my heart. Bennie loved you, Julianne, and he loved your father. What they say could not be true."

It broke Julianne's heart, as well. "I was told a deputy who has since retired did not believe Bennie had killed *Datt* and then taken his own life."

"Of course, Bennie would not do this. We had planned..." Emma's voice was thick with emotion. "You knew that we talked about marriage?"

Julianne nodded.

"Bennie was saving for our future. He wanted to buy land near your father so they could farm together and expand their property."

Emma glanced around as if fearing someone would overhear their conversation. Her face contorted. "I have to go."

Julianne caught her arm. "When can we talk?"

"Tomorrow afternoon. Mose and I were to visit relatives along with his parents. I'll pretend I'm not feeling well and beg to stay home."

Emma glanced back once again and then hurried into the grocery store. Julianne followed her friend's gaze. Mose Miller stood on the sidewalk near a buggy. His eyes narrowed, and his face twisted in an angry snarl.

Julie's heart pounded a warning.

"Let's go, William." She climbed behind the wheel and pulled away from Jones Grocery.

"What did Emma say?" William asked.

"It's what she didn't say that her body language told me loud and clear."

"What's that?" he asked.

"Emma fears her husband." Julianne

thought of the man who had attacked her the night she came back to Mountain Loft and the man who had been in her father's workshop. And again, the person who had broken into her house. With the way her pulse raced when she saw Mose and the fear she saw in Emma's eyes, she wondered if Mose could be involved.

Her brother never had liked Mose and thought he was out for his own good. Had Bennie met Mose that night, and was he the man who had killed her father and brother? Julianne needed to solve their deaths to be able to learn who was coming after her now. She didn't have proof, but a gut feeling told her the two situations were tied together, and she feared they involved Mose Miller. If that was true, Emma could be in danger.

If Mose was the killer, he had killed twice. If he killed twice, what would stop him from killing again?

Before leaving town, William and Julianne stopped at the sheriff's office, but he was still with the mayor.

"I wouldn't be surprised if the meeting lasts all day," the deputy admitted. "The sheriff said they had a lot to discuss."

Which William wished the deputy had mentioned earlier.

"I'd like to know what the sheriff thinks of Mose Miller," Julianne said as they drove toward William's farm.

"I saw Mose pass by your house the night after we saw him at the Country Kitchen."

"Was he in his buggy?" she asked.

William nodded. "Headed for the lake."

"Did you tell the deputy sheriff?"

"I was focused on your safety that night," Will admitted. "And not on some Amish guy riding by your property."

"Yet he could have been the man with the bandana."

"That's a possibility, but you need proof, Julie."

"I need to ask Emma where her husband was that night."

He held up his hand. "Just be careful of what you say. Emma loves Mose. If she thinks you're out to cause problems, she might be hesitant to share information."

"You didn't see the look on her face today."

"No, but if she fears her husband, she might be even more concerned about revealing anything that could incriminate him. Emma is a *gut* woman, and she loved your brother, but Mose is her husband."

Julianne sighed. "That's what's hard. To see her end up with a man she fears after what she had with Bennie. It doesn't seem fair."

She glanced again at William. "Emma said she would be alone tomorrow afternoon. Mose and his family plan to visit relatives. She'll make up an excuse to stay home. We could visit the sheriff after we see Emma."

Julianne hesitated for a moment. "That is if you're interested in going to town again."

He would go with Julianne, but he was concerned about Emma. Mose would be irate if he found them talking to his wife.

William kept worrying about both Emma's and Julianne's safety after they got home. Julianne helped her aunt in the kitchen for a few hours and then peered into the barn, where he was working.

"I'm driving to my house to hang the For Sale by Owner sign on the fencing," she called to him. "Aunt Mary said to be hungry tonight. She's cooking a huge meal, as if there were ten of us."

He laughed, hearing the playfulness in Julianne's voice. She had been so unsettled driving home and convinced Mose was involved in the attacks. Not that William thought Mose couldn't have been involved, but he wanted to give him the benefit of the doubt even if he was belligerent at times.

His treatment of Emma was more of a concern. Perhaps William should talk to one of the church leaders. The bishop, or even the deacon, could visit Mose and encourage him, as Scripture said, with fraternal correction to improve his attitude toward his wife.

Would it be enough to change his actions? William wasn't sure, but something needed to be done to keep both Emma Miller and Julianne safe.

TEN

Using a black marker, Julianne wrote her cell phone number on the For Sale sign. She retrieved a hammer and nails from her father's workshop and forced thoughts of a man wearing a bandana from her mind as she nailed the sign to her gate.

The air was cool and clouds blocked the sun. She wore only a sweater as a wrap and wished she had dressed more warmly.

Aunt Mary had left a few things behind last night due to their hurry to get to William's house. Julianne retrieved some of the items from the guest room and packed them in a tote before the sound of a car on the drive caused her to peer through the window.

A white sedan, clean and shining, as if it was brand-new, braked to a stop near the porch. Julianne ran downstairs.

Remembering the white car that had chased after her the night of her arrival as well as the SUV earlier today, she opened the kitchen door and stood poised on the threshold, ready to retreat inside and bolt the door if the visitor seemed threatening.

Her expression must have been less than welcoming as a tall man with dark, wavy hair and a well-trimmed beard stepped from the car and nodded a greeting. "Afternoon, ma'am. I hope I didn't startle you."

She waited for him to provide more information.

"I'm Ted McDonough, from Atlanta. I'm working with the mayor and some of the other good folks in Mountain Loft about a development I proposed to build. Brad Abbott mentioned your house and land was for sale."

"Aren't you a bit early?"

He smiled sheepishly. "You've talked to Brad. We're meeting tomorrow. I decided to drive up today and see the town for myself. In my line of work—it's good to know the area before I start talking money."

"What type of a development did you propose to the city?" Julianne knew the answer—a tract of homes. Julianne felt sure but she waited to hear what the developer would say.

"A few mountain homes for some of the folks in Atlanta who are ready to get out of the stress of city life."

"This is an Amish home, Mr. McDonough."

He held up his hand. "Call me Ted, please."

"An Amish home, Ted, means no central air or heating. No electricity or phone connections. I doubt the house would meet the standards of the *good* folks you have in mind." She accentuated the word *good* and then regretted her abrasive tone. For whatever reason, something about Ted stuck in her craw.

"I understand that renovations would need to be made to the house." He gazed at the surrounding farmland. "Brad said you've got sixty-five acres."

Mountain Loft's premier—and only— real-estate agent liked to tell all, even though Julianne hadn't agreed to work with him.

A satisfied smile crossed Ted's lips as he continued to peruse the land. "One-acre lots." He nodded, as if doing the math.

"Are you expecting an influx of people to the area, Ted?"

"Once the ski slope is developed. Then the lodge."

"Is there enough snow for skiing?"

"Artificial snow will augment anything Mother Nature doesn't provide. It's pricey, but people will pay." Ted rubbed his hands together as if anticipating the influx of revenue from all the ventures he had planned.

"Brad said Mountain Loft dates from the Georgia gold rush," he continued. "That local history will be a draw. I envision setting up a few sluice boxes in town where kids can pan for gold, as well as a replica of an old mine shaft and a historical museum."

He nodded again, his smile broadening. "I see the potential."

"Surely, you have other land to buy." She glanced at the Fulton County license plate that was as clean as his vehicle. "Did you happen to visit an abandoned farmhouse earlier this morning?"

"I just arrived in town. Brad said there are a number of parcels of land, although yours is the first I've visited. I'll talk to him tomorrow, and we'll come back probably in the afternoon, if that works for you."

She thought of meeting with Emma. "I won't be here until later in the day."

"Not a problem. Brad probably has a key to the house."

Not Brad, although someone did. "Why don't you talk to Brad? He can call me."

"Your number's on the sign."

"That's correct."

"How long have you had the house on the market?" Before she could answer, he continued, "You've made a wise decision to go with Brad. He has connections."

"So I've heard, but as the sign on my gate says, I'm selling the property myself and haven't entered into an agreement with Abbott Real Estate."

"For sale by owner is next to impossible." Which Brad had told her.

"I don't suppose I could take a peek inside the house today."

She held up her hand. "It's not a good time."

"Certainly, I understand." He rounded the front of his car and climbed the porch stairs.

Julianne had to fight the urge to slam the door in his face. He held out his hand and looked eager to make a connection. She accepted his handshake.

"Nice chatting with you, Ms. Graber."

"It's Julianne."

"I'll talk to Brad in the morning and he'll contact you."

"That sounds like a plan."

"Have a good night."

Julianne hoped she would.

As Ted pulled out of the drive, she realized her mistake. She should have told the developer she wasn't listing her property with Abbott Real Estate, although she wanted to talk to Brad first. Did everyone expect her to sell her farm to the first buyer, especially someone who was interested in cutting up good farmland for home development?

The farm had been in her family for three generations. She wanted to find a buyer, but the right buyer.

"What did he want?"

William startled her.

"I saw the white sedan in your drive and thought you might want some company."

She patted her chest, hoping her heart would stop racing. "You scared me nearly to death."

"Was the guy asking directions?"

"He was asking to buy my property."

William glanced at the sign. "Evidently the For Sale sign worked."

"But I'm not selling."

He smiled. "You're staying on the farm?"

She shook her head. "I'm selling, but not to him."

"Because?"

She told him about Ted McDonough's plans to divide her farm into small parcels of land. "I'm surprised the mayor is so eager to expand the town."

"The mayor's getting his real-estate license and plans to work with Brad Abbott on the side."

"You've heard that?"

William nodded. "Nothing is a secret in Mountain Loft."

Except the identity of the man or men who wanted to scare her away from her home.

"So the mayor has a personal interest in developing some of the rural areas?" she said. "More homes to sell and commissions to make. I wonder how many folks will go along with the idea."

"I've heard a few Amish guys talk about investing their money."

"In real estate?"

Will shrugged. "It's an option."

"Would they sell their farms?"

"Some of the younger Amish families are moving on to other areas. Mountain farming can be difficult. Winters are rough. The growing season is longer in the southern part of the state, better weather, better return on their money and their labor."

"Young people leave town and the parents want to move to where the kids live."

"Or move to town and live off their investments."

"It seems counter-Amish," said Julianne.

"Things change with time. Land is scarce in some areas so the Amish are moving, relocating."

"What about you, William?"

"I'm staying here. Mountain Loft is my home."

"For seventeen years, I thought it was my home, too." What William had said was true. Times change and so had she, although now that she was back home, she was unsettled about her future. The *Englisch* life had been alluring. To have her own apartment and car. To wear *fancy* clothes, although she had stayed clear of flashy colors or less-than-modest attire. Seeing Aunt Mary in her homemade dress and apron brought back so many memories—good memories—of her *mamm*.

"I need to get some of Aunt Mary's things

from upstairs, then I'll lock up and head back to your house."

"I'll wait for you, Julianne."

She appreciated William's protectiveness.

Leaving him on the porch, she hurried upstairs and grabbed a shawl her aunt had left in the guest room and the tote Julie had packed earlier. Her phone rang, which surprised her. Expecting to hear the sheriff's voice or Brad Abbott's, she raised the cell to her ear.

"Julianne, this is Ted McDonough again. Look, I had a thought and wanted to run it by you before I got too far away from your farm. I planned on grabbing an early dinner in town before checking into my room at the B and B and wondered if you would care to join me."

"Join you?" Was he talking about taking her out to dinner?

"I've never been to Mountain Loft and don't know where to find a good meal. I hate eating alone and thought it would be enjoyable to get to know you better. That is, if you're not busy."

He *was* asking her out.

"The Country Kitchen has good food," she said. "There were a few other restaurants when I lived here previously, but I've been away for a few years."

"The Country Kitchen works for me," he assured her. "I'll turn around and be back at your place in five minutes or so. If that gives you enough time."

"Mr. McDonough—Ted—I already have plans for dinner." With her Aunt Mary and William. "But you'll find a nice selection of dishes on the menu that should suit your fancy."

"We'll get together another time then."

Or maybe not.

"I'll talk to Brad in the morning," he continued. "We'll be in touch."

If Brad called tomorrow, she would set him straight. If only she could warn the *good people* in town, as Ted had called them, that having a large influx of city folks move to Mountain Loft would change the town's character. She'd heard the old-timers in Dahlonega bemoan the growth in their town as they reminisced about the past.

Although a town, just like a family, couldn't go back. She had grieved for her father and brother and had wanted to turn back time in hopes of stopping the tragedy from happening. In hindsight, she wouldn't have told her father that Bennie and William were meeting that night. She had known her father would be upset, to say the least. Had she set him up? Or was she trying to prove something to her brother? That she was someone of worth? After her mother's death, that had been important to her. Probably because she felt both men blamed her for spreading the illness that claimed *Mamm*'s life.

Unwilling to dwell on the painful past, Julianne hurried downstairs and found William waiting for her where she'd left him on the porch.

"Everything okay?" he asked.

"Everything's fine." Except it wasn't. Not when someone wanted to do her harm.

She locked the kitchen door and hurried

to the car. William opened the door for her and then rounded to the passenger side after she was behind the wheel.

Glancing at the For Sale by Owner sign, her stomach rolled. How much time did she did have to sell her farm? Her boss in Dahlonega said he'd hold her job, but she would eventually need to get back to work. She thought of the welcome committee that had attacked her the night she arrived home and then returned the following night, and the break-in the night after that, too. Staying in Mountain Loft might be dangerous to her health, as well as her life.

Perhaps she needed to give Ted's offer more thought, but one thing was certain as she glanced at William. She had made the right decision about declining Ted's dinner offer. Sitting across from William tonight as they enjoyed Aunt Mary's delicious meal would be far more pleasant than making small talk with a developer from the city. Ted McDonough was tall and muscular, like the burglar who had broken into her house. Plus, he drove a white car.

Turning into the Lavy drive, she forced the thoughts from her mind. Ted was full of himself, but otherwise he seemed like a decent guy, even if he had been insistent about buying her land.

Aunt Mary stepped onto the porch as Julianne braked to a stop. "The meal is ready for those who I hope are hungry."

"That would be me," William said.

After parking her car in the barn, she and William hurried inside and inhaled the rich scent of stew wafting from the woodstove. Before William closed the door behind them, she heard the clip-clop of a horse's hooves and glanced outside to see a man dressed in black with a black beard pass by on the road. His gaze was on her farmhouse. He pulled his buggy to a stop in front of the drive and leaned down as if to read the For Sale sign before he flicked the reins.

William stepped closer. "Seems you have someone else interested in your farm."

"Who is it? Can you tell?"

He nodded. His tone was sharp when he

spoke. "I recognize the man in the buggy. You've seen him before. It's Mose Miller."

A thread of worry wrapped around her heart. Mose Miller wore black, had anger issues and had disliked Bennie, and seemed to dislike William, as well. Did he also dislike her? And, if so, would he do her harm so he could lay claim to her farm?

"We'll visit Emma tomorrow," she said, her voice low.

Just so Mose wouldn't see them. No telling what he would do if he realized Emma had disobeyed him. Would he hurt his wife, or would he take his upset out on Julianne? If Mose had been the man who had attacked Julianne before, what would stop him from attacking her again?

ELEVEN

The next day, William couldn't shrug off his concern about visiting the Miller home. "Are you sure Mose and his parents will be away from the house?" he asked Julianne as she slipped into her jacket and wrapped a scarf about her neck.

"Emma said they would visit friends throughout the afternoon, Will."

"Still, it has me worried."

Julianne guided the car along the narrow country road. "We'll drive by the Miller farm to make certain Mose and his parents aren't home. If the coast is clear, we can turn around and go back."

Passing the house, they both stared at the barn and outbuildings, then at the pastures and fields surrounding the house. "I don't see anyone," Julianne said. She made a U-turn and headed back to the entrance to the Miller farm.

William continued to study the area as they pulled into the drive. "Let's make this a short visit. Meeting Emma in town might have been a better option."

Julianne parked on the far side of the house so the car wouldn't be seen by anyone passing by on the road. News traveled fast in the Amish community. Neither of them wanted Mose or his parents to learn that Emma had visitors while they were gone.

The door of the farmhouse opened as they stepped from the car. Emma motioned them inside. "I wondered if you would remember."

"Of course," Julianne said. "But we wanted to make certain you were alone."

They hurried into the sparsely furnished home. The two women hugged as William closed the door. "Mose is gone?" he asked.

"*Yah*, he and his parents left earlier than planned, but I do not expect them to return until nightfall." She pointed to the table.

"Sit, please. Would you care for a cup of coffee?"

"No, I am fine," William said and Julianne nodded in agreement.

Once seated, Julianne slipped out of her coat and scarf, then grabbed her friend's hand. "I am worried about you, Emma. Mose seems upset every time I see him."

"He and his father have argued recently. Tension in the house is high. His mother says nothing that goes against her husband, but she is on edge, as well. Mose wants to move, but we need land and a house. He hopes to do this before the baby comes."

"He's driven by Julianne's farm a few times," William said. "On his way to the lake."

Emma nodded. "He mentioned your property, but we would need to get a loan through the bank. He had hoped his father would provide a few thousand dollars for a down payment, but the two argued over that. His father does not understand why we want to leave."

"What about building a separate house here on the farm, which is what most Amish families do? You would have your own space," William suggested.

"Except his father claims he does not have the cash needed to buy the wood and building supplies at this time and insists we wait until after harvest, yet that would be months from now and there is little room here. When the baby comes we will not even have space for a crib in our tiny bedroom."

Emma was visibly upset, and William hated to increase her angst, but a question needed to be asked. "Mose has passed my house and Julie's a number of times on his way to the lake. Why does he go there so often in the evening?"

"My husband enjoys fishing, but during the day he works with his *datt* on the farm. In the evening, he likes to have some time for himself. Often he comes home with trout and bass."

"Yet he leaves you with his family?" Julianne rubbed Emma's arm.

"Sometimes…" She looked embarrassed and hung her head. "Sometimes it is better when he is not here."

"Oh, Emma, you are making me even more worried," Julianne said. "What brought you and Mose together?"

Emma shook her head. "I was broken-hearted after Bennie died." She glanced up. Her eyes glistened with tears. "What the sheriff said was not true. Bennie loved your father. He would never have harmed your *datt* or himself."

"Remember we were all at the lake that night," William said. "What happened after you and Bennie left?"

"He took me home so he could meet with someone about a business deal." She glanced at Julianne. "I thought you knew?"

"I did, but I believed he and William planned to meet."

Emma's brow furrowed. "William had nothing to do with this. It was someone else. Bennie had been excited about an opportunity to make money that had come about a few weeks earlier, but when he looked into this business endeavor, he realized there were problems."

"What kind of problems?" William asked.

"He didn't say, but he told me he was gathering evidence."

Julianne leaned closer. "Evidence makes me think of something illegal."

Emma nodded. "Bennie said what he had uncovered was upsetting. He planned to make the information known."

"To whom?" Julianne asked.

Emma shrugged. "I wish I knew. I should have pressed for more details, but I was worried. Bennie had purchased a gun." She glanced at Julianne. "Did he tell you?"

Julianne shook her head. "I did not know at the time, but buying a gun meant Bennie was concerned about his own safety. He must have thought the person he planned to meet could be dangerous."

"That is why I was afraid," Emma said. "I told him to go to the bishop."

"Did he?"

"Not that I know of."

"Did you see the information Bennie had collected?"

"He did not want me to get involved, but

he assured me he had copies of records that would prove what he claimed was true."

"Where did he keep the records?"

"He never told me and I did not ask." Emma hesitated a moment. "But there is something else you need to know."

"What is it, Emma?" Julianne squeezed her friend's hand.

"When your Aunt Mary took you to Willkommen so you could get away, she asked me to look after the house and gave me a key. She was so upset that day I doubt she remembers."

Julianne glanced at William. "You had a key to my father's house?"

Emma nodded. "I would have returned it earlier, but you and Aunt Mary never came back. From what she told people, you didn't want visitors."

"Thank you for holding on to it."

"Yet there is a problem."

"What kind of problem, Emma?"

"I kept the key in a trunk in my room. When I looked for it earlier today, it was not there."

"Did anyone else know about the key?"

"I told no one." She thought for a moment and then her face twisted. "That is not right. Someone else did know."

Julianne raised her brow. "Mose knew, didn't he?"

Emma nodded. "He saw it soon after we married. I told him I planned to return it when I next saw you, but you never came back."

The sound of a buggy caused Emma's face to blanch. She hurried to the window. "Mose is returning early."

Racing back to the table, she motioned them toward the door. "You must leave now."

"If you feel threatened, come to my house, Emma," William said. "You will be safe with us."

"I am grateful you came to my rescue last week, William. You made Mose realize he needed to treat me better, at least when we were in town. So thank you."

She squeezed Julianne's hand. "Take the dirt path through the woods. It leads to the old back trail. If you leave by the main road, Mose will see you."

Julianne hugged Emma, then grabbed her coat and scarf and hurried, along with William, to the car. Thick woods covered the rear of the property, but her car would be visible for about thirty seconds before they entered the densest section of the forest. If only Mose wouldn't see them.

Mose had passed by Julianne's house the night she had been attacked. Someone broke into the house the next night and had used a key. The only spare key anyone knew about had been in Emma's trunk, which would be easy for Mose to retrieve.

Was Mose looking for something or did he want to scare Julianne off the property? Or was there another reason for him entering the farmhouse? Did Mose Miller want to do Julianne harm?

"Mose Miller is the man in the bandana," Julianne said to William as they left the forest and turned onto the back path to town. "I need to tell the sheriff."

"I thought you were upset with Sheriff Taylor."

"I am, but he needs to know that Mose has a key to my house."

Once they arrived in Mountain Loft, she parked in a rear lot not far from the sheriff's office, draped her scarf around her neck and climbed from the car. Gloria pulled into a parking spot next to them.

"William, I need to talk to you." Brad Abbott's receptionist seemed breathless as she stepped to the pavement.

"Can it wait, Gloria?"

"It'll only take a minute." She titled her head and put her hands together as if pleading with him. "Please!"

He turned to Julianne. "Go ahead and talk to the sheriff. I'll join you in a few minutes."

Gloria still liked William—Julianne could see it—but with her tight skirts and stiletto heels, she hardly looked suited for a life on an Amish farm. Maybe she thought Will would leave the faith. At one time, Julianne had thought that, too, but Will seemed content farming his land and abiding by the

Ordnung. Gloria needed to focus her attention on Ralph Reynolds instead of an Amish man who needed to marry within the faith.

Julianne needed to keep that in mind, as well, lest she become overly attracted to the handsome farmer. She still harbored feelings for him that had started in their youth. Being with Will these last few days had made her even more aware that he was a good and righteous man. He was also considerate and compassionate, and when he looked at her, her cheeks burned and her pulse raced.

Once again, she recalled the intensity of his gaze and the warmth of his embrace when they were at the lake so long ago. Thoughts of his kiss filled her mind as she rounded the corner. An alleyway veered off to the left. On the road ahead, she spied a garbage truck heading toward her. The truck's trash compactor was activated. The clatter drowned out any other noise and sent her thoughts of William fleeing as she eased into the alley to elude the rickety truck's approach.

Grimacing at the racket, she closed her eyes for an instant. A hand grabbed her arm. Her eyes popped open. She tried to jerk her arm free. His grip tightened even more.

"Help," she screamed. "Help me!" The sound of her cry was drowned out by the whirl of the trash compactor.

The man pulled her against his chest. He was tall and bulky, and the sleeves of his shirt were black. Out of the corner of her eye, she saw a red bandana.

"Why didn't you leave town?" the guy snarled.

His breath soured her stomach. She jammed her elbow in his side and kicked his shin. His hands tightened even more.

He dragged her deeper into the alley.

Where's William?

Her heart pounded, and she thrashed to free herself.

He wrapped his left arm around her neck. She clawed at his forearm to break his hold. His arm pressed on her windpipe. She needed air. Now.

Her limbs grew heavy. She tried to fight,

but her mind was groggy. *Stay alert*, she told herself.

The palm of the man's right hand pushed on the back of her head. Her lungs were on fire. Her vision blurred.

Metal scraped against metal. The grating sound made her heart pound all the more.

Her limbs went weak, and she slumped into darkness.

Seconds—or maybe minutes—later, she slipped back into consciousness and blinked her eyes open. She was lying on her side. Her hand grasped something wet and slimy, and the putrid stench of garbage made her stomach roll.

A narrow shaft of light filtered into the metal container. At the far side of the enclosure, she saw small beady eyes, whiskers and a long tail.

A scream welled up in her throat just as the lid on the trash receptacle slammed shut, trapping her inside.

The rat scurried over her leg. She tried to scream, but no sound came out. She raised her hand and pounded against the side of the Dumpster. Her attempt was drown out by the insistent roar of the garbage truck.

William was with Gloria. The sheriff was in his office, and she would be tossed, along with a Dumpster full of refuse, into the garbage truck. Her last thoughts were of William and whether he would find her crushed to death in the trash compactor.

TWELVE

"There's nothing going on between us, Gloria," William said as he tried to distance himself from the receptionist. They had been friends in their youth. Maybe a little more than friends for a few weeks. Gloria had wanted him to leave the faith then, and he had made no pretense of his desire to remain Amish ever since he returned home to care for his father.

Excusing himself, he hurried to the sheriff's office. Deputy O'Reilly was at the desk.

"Is Julianne with the sheriff?"

"The sheriff's meeting with the mayor."

"Julianne hasn't been here?" William's stomach tightened. "She parked in the rear lot. Something happened between there and here."

O'Reilly followed Will outside. They hurried to her car and then raced around the side of the building.

William spied her scarf on the ground beside the Dumpster.

A garbage truck backed into the alley.

His heart nearly stopped, and he ran toward the truck. "No!"

O'Reilly followed. "What'd you see?"

"Her scarf. Something tells me—"

Nearing the truck, he pounded on the driver's door. "Stop the truck. I want to check that receptacle before you throw the garbage in the hopper."

The guy peered from the window. "Hey, buddy, I've got a job to do."

"I hear ya, but the deputy sheriff wants you to cut your engine and give it a break."

The guy looked at O'Reilly and shrugged. "Whatever."

William ran to the Dumpster. The lid was closed. "Give me a hand," he called to both men.

The truck driver jumped from his cab and hustled to where they stood. "You guys want to tell me what you're looking for?"

"Just help us lift the lid."

Working together, the three of them raised the metal top and pushed it back. William climbed to the top of the receptacle and looked down. His heart nearly stopped.

Julianne was lying on a pile of garbage. He jumped into the bin and placed his hand on her neck.

"She's got a pulse."

Lifting her into his arms, he held her close for a second and then passed her over the top of the container to the deputy. The stench was terrible, and his feet sunk into the refuse.

"Looks like a rodent bite on her leg. Call the paramedics."

An ambulance arrived in less than three minutes. William's heart pounded. She was pale and unresponsive.

"We'll take her to the clinic," the lead EMT said. "The doc will decide whether she needs to go to the hospital." They loaded her into the ambulance.

William retrieved Julianne's purse from

the Dumpster and climbed in beside her. "I'm catching a ride."

The sirens screamed as the ambulance raced to the medical clinic on the outskirts of town.

William held her hand. "Come on, Julianne. Open your eyes. Tell me you're okay."

William never should have talked to Gloria. Had she pulled him away from Julianne on purpose? Her comments about still wanting to be together had seemed foolish, unless she had distracted Will so someone could attack Julianne.

As soon as they arrived at the clinic, she was wheeled into a treatment room. William had to remain in the waiting area. He paced the floor, and then met O'Reilly outside when the deputy pulled his patrol car to the door.

"Find Gloria and ask her what's going on," William demanded. "Then find Ralph Reynolds. He could have done this. He's got a chip on his shoulder and is as rotten as his brothers."

"Anyone else?"

"If you see Mose Miller in town, haul him in, too. He had access to a key to Julie's house and could have broken in. Someone did this to Julianne and I want to know who and why."

Will retrieved the car keys from Julianne's purse. "Can someone drive her car to the clinic?"

O'Reilly nodded. "Roger that. I'll get the keys back to you. Tell the clinic to call me as soon as the doc has any information."

Information, William thought, like what would have happened if he hadn't seen her scarf. A minute later and the Dumpster would have dumped its load into the back of the truck and then the huge crushing arm of the compactor would have activated. As the garbage was crushed, Julianne would have been, as well.

"From what you've told me, it sounds like some kind of a choke hold made you pass out," Dr. Norris told Julianne.

Her head pounded and she was queasy, and every time she thought of the rat, she wanted to draw her legs to her chest and huddle in the corner.

"You were fortunate," the doctor said.

"You call it fortunate to have been tossed in a trash heap?" The doc wasn't making sense.

"Fortunate you weren't crushed in the compactor. Seems someone wanted to do you harm. The good thing is the garbage truck stopped before he cleared the Dumpster."

"I tried to fight, but I couldn't move."

"Do you feel like talking to the sheriff?"

"Only if I have to."

The doc smiled. "He's in the waiting room. William Lavy is there, too. He's pacing like a mountain lion ready to attack. I've never seen an Amish man so rattled and so angry. I should take his blood pressure to make sure he doesn't have a cardiac arrest."

"Evidently he's worried about me." She wanted to smile, but her head hurt too much.

"I noticed those scrapes and bruises that are a few days old. You want to tell me what's going on."

She explained about coming home and the

man in black waiting for her the first two nights and the burglar the third night.

Dr. Norris rubbed his jaw. "Someone didn't want you to come back to Mountain Loft."

"That's what it seems."

"You need to take care of yourself, Julianne. I can't let you go back to a lonely farmhouse at the end of desolate two-lane road. Not after what's happened to you."

"William contacted my aunt, and she's staying with me."

"Still, two women can't do much against a man, even if you think you can."

"My aunt and I are staying at William's house, but I don't want the information to get around town. In the meantime, I'm trying to sell my farm so I can move back to Dahlonega."

"Maybe you should move back ahead of schedule. Surely Brad Abbott could take care of the sale."

"I'm not interested in listing with Mr. Abbott. He seems to think Mountain Loft needs home development and a lot of newcomers."

The doc nodded. "That's the mayor's plan. A number of folks in town are opposed to what's in the works."

"Do you think the person who attacked me might have something to do with the housing project?"

"You'll have to run that by the sheriff. If you start feeling worse or develop a fever, contact me immediately. You have a cell phone?"

She nodded. "I do, although reception can be sketchy."

"Then have William bring you into the clinic if things go south."

"I'm almost afraid to ask what bit me." She glanced at her bandaged leg. "I keep seeing a rat, but maybe I was dreaming. Long tail, beady eyes."

"I doubt that was a dream. You need a tetanus shot."

She groaned.

"Rat bite fever is another complication. That's why I want you to call the clinic if you have a fever, develop a rash or have achy joints."

"The rat may do more damage than the man in black," she said, trying to joke, but she wasn't laughing.

After she had the shot and talked to the sheriff, the doctor released her. William was waiting for her in the hallway. He held up her keys. "I'll drive home."

"What will the bishop say?"

"He knows I can drive a car. Remember that accident I was in as a teen."

"When my father forbid Bennie from inviting you into our home. Look, I'm sorry this happened."

"Julianne, it wasn't your fault. I'm to blame for getting sidelined by Gloria. If I'd been with you, I doubt the guy would have grabbed you."

"The only person to blame is the guy with the red bandana. Let's get back to your house so we can ensure Aunt Mary is okay."

"She'll be worried about you, just like I am."

For all the lightness she tried to add to her voice, Julianne was worried, too. The guy who was after her seemed more determined than ever to do her harm.

THIRTEEN

After explaining to Aunt Mary what had happened in town, William settled Julianne in a comfortable chair near the woodstove and then went outside to check the surrounding area. He ran to the Graber farm and tried the doors to ensure they were still locked. Glancing in the windows, he saw that everything looked neat and orderly, including the workshop and other outbuildings. The assailant had been in town and not at Julianne's property.

William would have to be vigilant in the days ahead to keep Julianne safe. He had let her out of his sight, and the man had grabbed her. From now on, William needed to stay with Julianne, although he doubted she would be pleased with a full-time bodyguard.

The next morning, he heard a buggy and

left the barn to see who was approaching. A woman guided her mare into the drive. He approached the rig and was relieved to see Rachel Hochstetler Krause. She and Julianne had been good friends in their youth, and Rachel had driven Julie home from the lake the night her father and brother had died.

"I heard Julianne has returned home and thought I might find her here," Rachel said, her smile bright.

"Did you go to the Graber farm first?"

"After what happened yesterday, William, I did not think you would let her stay alone."

"Her Aunt Mary is here, as well, although both woman were determined to remain at the Graber farmhouse at first."

"Julianne hasn't changed, *yah*? She wants to handle everything without help. She is independent for an Amish woman."

"She has left the faith, Rachel."

The old friend nodded. "This, I have heard."

Rachel climbed from the buggy and followed William inside. Julianne was in the kitchen working with Aunt Mary.

"It has been so long," Julianne said as she hugged her friend. "You know my aunt."

"Of course. I'm glad you could be with Julianne now." Rachel placed a plastic container filled with cookies on the counter and smiled. "I baked these this morning."

"Which is so thoughtful. It is *gut* to see you, Rachel." Mary motioned the younger women to the table. "Sit while I prepare a bit of cake to have with a cup of coffee, *yah*? Or perhaps you would prefer your cookies."

"Cake sounds *wunderbaar*." Rachel sat next to Julianne, then lowered her head. "I wanted to see you after you left Mountain Loft with your aunt, but my *datt* forbid me to go to Willkommen. Although I have always been a dutiful daughter, I regret not going against his wishes." She glanced up and took Julianne's hand. "Can you ever forgive me?"

"You have nothing for which to apologize. I was not myself for a long period." She glanced at her aunt. "Aunt Mary insisted

I stay away from Mountain Loft and from anyone who might stir up memories from the past."

"Perhaps I am the one who was wrong," Mary said as she placed the plated cake before both women. "In hindsight, my desire to protect you, Julianne, went too far." She glanced at William. "I was seeing the situation through my own grief and probably delayed your healing because of my overzealous desire to keep you safe."

Julianne grabbed her aunt's hand. "We were both stumbling in the dark, but we survived." She turned back to Rachel and squeezed her hand. "Today is a new day."

"With new problems," Rachel added. "From what I have heard in town."

William poured coffee into four mugs and took them to the table. "What are people saying?"

"That Julianne was attacked and thrown in a garbage container near the sheriff's office." She shivered. "They also said you were bitten by a rat."

"Yet I survived, thanks to William. He found me just in time."

Rachel smiled at William. "For this I am grateful."

"How is Eli?" William asked. Rachel's husband was a hardworking farmer. They had married while William was away from the faith, and Eli had been quick to welcome William back into the community.

"He said to tell you hello and looks forward to seeing you soon."

"I always liked Eli," Julianne said, "although I did not realize you two were attracted to each other."

Rachel shrugged. "Time changes the way we look at things...and at people, *yah*?"

Julianne glanced at William for a moment, which warmed his heart.

"There is more cake," Aunt Mary said once she had finished her own cup of coffee.

"Thank you, but this is plenty," Rachel said with a smile.

"Then I will leave you and go upstairs."

As soon as Mary left, Julianne turned to

Rachel. "I have wanted to talk to you about the night you dropped me at home."

Rachel shook her head. "I should have gone inside with you."

"You did not need to be exposed to what had happened." Julianne hesitated for a moment and then asked, "Did you notice anything strange after you left my house?"

Rachel nodded and leaned closer to Julianne. "I took the old back road, thinking I would not see anyone." She turned to William. "It was late and my parents expected me home earlier, yet I knew they would be asleep, and I did not want anyone to tell them their daughter had been driving home late at night."

"Who did you see?" Julianne asked.

"No one that I could recognize. It was a vehicle. Which surprised me, since usually cars take the main road and only buggies use the back path. I was frightened when I heard the car and saw the headlights so I hid the buggy behind a small rise off to the side of the road."

"The car passed you by?"

"*Yah*, the driver was going fast, especially for the old road. The moon was behind the clouds and broke out only for a few minutes so I could see as the car passed."

"What can you tell us about the car?" William asked.

"It was not big and not small—a medium-size car." Rachel shrugged apologetically. "I know little about *Englisch* vehicles."

"And the color of the vehicle?"

"That is something I know for sure. The moon came out as it passed by. The car was white."

"White?" Julianne asked. "You're sure?"

She nodded. "*Yah*, for this I am certain."

A white car like the car that had come after Julianne the night she had returned to Mountain Loft.

Nothing made sense. Would the person who had been at the house five years ago return on the night Julianne returned home? And if so, why?

Julianne's cell phone rang later that day when she and Aunt Mary were working in the kitchen. She looked at the monitor and spied Brad Abbott's name. Checking her phone log, she realized he had called twice earlier.

"I didn't hear my phone when you called," she said after exchanging greetings. "Service can be spotty this far from town."

"Tell me about it. Showing property at the high elevations becomes difficult when I'm trying to contact an interested buyer who needs directions."

"Were you out by the old quarry yesterday?"

"No, why?"

Because he drove a white SUV like the car that had turned in front of them. "I saw a car that looked like yours."

"White SUVs are popular."

Which she knew too well. "Did you need something?"

He hesitated, then got to the point of his call. "Ted McDonough's with me. He said he ran into you yesterday and from what he saw of your property, he's interested."

"Brad—"

"We've been looking at some land not far from your farm and thought we'd stop. I've got the papers ready for the listing. We talked about price the other day."

"Brad, I—"

"You're breaking up. Give us fifteen minutes and we'll be pulling into your driveway."

The call ended. She stared at the phone and shook her head. Brad Abbott usually got his way, or so it seemed. Ted McDonough probably did, as well.

She told her aunt about the high-pressure real-estate agent. "I'll meet him in the drive and politely explain that I don't need his services."

"Maybe William should go with you."

"He's in the far pasture. I don't want to disturb him, and I won't be gone long."

Julianne walked to her house, happy for the exercise and relieved that she could finally tell Brad Abbott that she wasn't dealing with him. The men pulled into her drive soon after she arrived at the house. Mud caked the wheels of Brad's vehicle, but the license plate was clean and easy to read.

They exited the car and nodded in greeting. "Just inhale that fresh air," Brad said to the Atlanta developer. "You won't find that in the city."

"That's why folks want to move to Mountain Loft." Ted smiled at her and held out his hand. "Good to see you, Julianne. Thanks for that tip about the Country Kitchen. Good food and plenty of it." He patted his slim stomach. Ted probably ran five miles a day and lifted weights.

"I'm glad you enjoyed the meal."

"The only thing better would be to have enjoyed your company. I hope you'll be free another night, maybe this evening."

"I'm afraid—"

Brad grabbed the papers and held them out to her, along with a pen. "I need your signature, Julianne, then we're in business. We can show Ted the house and walk some of the property. I picked up a plat map from city hall."

He turned and looked at the gate. "I'll pull

down that For Sale by Owner sign while you read over the real-estate agreement."

As he started toward the gate, she grabbed his arm. "Brad, stop."

He looked puzzled and raised his brow. "Is there a problem?"

"I visited your office yesterday."

"Gloria told me. I was meeting with the mayor. We talked about your property. Ted met the mayor this morning. He's excited about what this development will mean for Mountain Loft. A number of the businessmen in town are, as well."

"And some aren't excited, Brad. I doubt you'll find the Amish enthused about the endeavor."

He shook his head. "The Amish I've talked to are eager to sell. They're ready to retire, and the money Ted can offer will make their golden years a dream come true."

"The Amish don't dream of retirement like the *Englisch*. They continue working, and I'm surprised they're talking about selling their farms, especially with how difficult good farmland is to find these days."

"You've been away for a long time, Julianne. Things change."

Which everyone kept telling her.

"I've got an idea," Ted said. "Why don't you read over the real-estate agreement and meet us in town tonight. The bed and breakfast is serving a private dinner that Brad arranged. The mayor and his wife will be there, along with some of the other people involved in seeing the town grow."

He looked at Brad. "You could add another person, I'm sure."

"Of course." Brad's face brightened. "That's a great idea. Join us at six, Julianne. You know the B and B?"

"No, but I'm sure I could find it, except I'm not interested, Brad."

"Then we'll stop by tomorrow or you can stop by my office if you come to town."

She handed the papers back to him. "I'm not interested in signing with your real-estate firm."

"What are you saying?"

"This farm is being sold by the owner."

She pointed to the sign on the gate and then back at herself. "That's me, Brad."

Turning to Ted, she said, "Thank you for your interest in my property, but I'm not selling my land to a developer, and I'm not joining you for dinner. Now, gentlemen, I'd like you to leave my farm."

Brad's eyes bulged. "You've got to be joking."

She leveled her gaze at him. "No joke, Brad."

Ted shook his head. "Why did you lead me on, Brad? The mayor will hear about this."

They climbed into the white SUV, still grumbling.

Julianne hadn't felt this good in ages.

From the other side of the road, she saw Will. He hurried to join her as the two men drove back to town.

"Are you okay?" he asked, concern covering his face. "Did they cause any problems?"

"None whatsoever. I told them I was not selling my property to a developer from Atlanta. I don't think they liked my decision, but they left and that makes me happy."

Although her elation was tempered by the thought of the driver of a white car who had chased after her that first night home. As much as she wanted to remain upbeat, she wondered if either Brad or Ted, since both drove white vehicles, would be coming back tonight or some other night to teach her a lesson.

She was thankful to have William on her side. Working together, they'd be able to outsmart the man in the bandana, whoever he was. At least, that was her hope. Still, she needed to be careful so she could stay safe.

And William? She wanted him to be safe, too.

The sound of another vehicle turned their attention to the road. A beige delivery van with the words Jones Grocery on the side pulled into the drive.

Harvey braked to a stop and waved in greeting as he climbed from behind the wheel. "I heard what happened in town, Julianne, and wanted to check on you myself."

Touched by his concern, she smiled at the sweet man who had always held a warm place in her heart. "I had a little run-in with someone who doesn't want me here."

"That's what I heard. Does the sheriff have any leads?"

"He's investigating." Although she wondered how long it would take Sheriff Taylor to come up with a suspect.

Harvey shook his head. "I told Nancy I'm worried about you, living out so far and all alone."

"Aunt Mary came to stay with me." Julianne glanced at William and smiled ever so slightly.

"Bless your aunt. Which reminds me..." Harvey opened the side door to the van and retrieved a large basket filled with fresh fruit. "Nancy and I thought this might brighten your day."

"Oh, Harvey!" Tears stung her eyes in response to their thoughtfulness. She blinked them back and hugged the good-hearted grocer before accepting the basket filled with an assortment of fruit—apples and oranges, mangoes and kiwis, as well as a pine-apple. The pretty basket was topped with a royal blue bow.

"You shouldn't have, but I'm so grateful. Thank you, Harvey, and be sure to give Nancy my thanks, as well."

"We hated to learn that someone attacked you so viciously. You can't stay here, Julianne, even if Aunt Mary is with you."

Hearing the concern in his tone, she wanted to reassure the kindly grocer. "William lives close by if we need help."

Harvey nodded to William as if he'd just realized he was there. "I made an offer that first day you came into my shop and it still holds, Julianne. Let me handle the sale of your property. You go back to Dahlonega. I'll keep you updated on any buyers." He hesitated for a moment. "Or I could buy it myself."

"You're too kind, Harvey. As much as I appreciate your offer, you have a business to run in town, and I want to sell the farm on my own."

She owed it to her father.

"Would you like to come inside for a cup of tea?" she asked. "I could cut the pineapple. It looks ripe."

"I need to get back to town. Nancy's minding the store, and I told her I wouldn't be long."

"Thank her for me, Harvey. The basket of fruit was very thoughtful."

"You're special to us, Julianne." He smiled ruefully. "I can still remember how you and Anna used to skip along the sidewalk, your hair flying in the breeze, cute as peanuts."

The memory tugged at her heart. "Anna was a good friend."

"It's hard to know why things happen. I worked to provide for my family and then in the blink of an eye everything changes."

Glancing at her with doleful eyes, he added, "I don't have to tell you about life changing. Stop by the grocery when you get to town. Nancy would enjoy seeing you again."

He waved goodbye and then climbed into his delivery van and pulled onto the road.

William stepped closer and took the basket from Julianne's hands. "Let me carry that for you."

She nodded her thanks and stared wistfully after the grocery van. "With my own *datt* gone, Harvey's about the closest thing to a father I have."

"He'd be touched to hear you say that, Julie, especially since he and Nancy lost their own daughter."

"Life isn't fair, Will."

"*Gott* did not promise fairness, but He said we should pick up our crosses and follow Him. Some crosses are heavier than others."

"In my opinion, they're all hard to carry."

All she had ever wanted was for her *datt* to be proud of her. Instead his gaze always held a bit of sadness when he looked at her. Probably because of her resemblance to her *mamm.* If Julianne hadn't gotten sick, her mother never would have died.

Life wasn't fair, as she had told William, and bad things happened. She had lost her mother, father and brother, and for the rest of her life, Julianne would always feel responsible for their deaths.

* * *

William knew Julianne was troubled and overwrought with emotion. His heart went out to her.

"Before we head back," she said, "will you help me search Bennie's room once again?"

"For the information he gathered about the shady business deal?"

She nodded. "I want to make certain we didn't miss anything that might still be there. If only I had some clue about the man who wanted to go into business with him?"

"Bennie knew a lot of folks in town because of working at the grocery. He knew things I never heard about on the farm. I remember a couple of *Englisch* guys were hanging around a few months earlier. They had grandiose ideas about starting a business."

"Did Bennie consider joining them?"

"He did, until they headed north to Tennessee."

"Who were the men?"

"They were brothers. Greg and Hank, but I can't remember their last name."

He kept thinking about the twosome as he followed Julianne into the house. Leaving the basket on the kitchen table, he climbed the stairs and joined her in Bennie's room.

"Didn't we just do this?" He chuckled as they searched the dresser drawers and blanket chest.

"We did, but we were looking for my *datt*'s money. Now we need business papers, maybe spreadsheets or a file folder with printouts."

"Did your dad have a computer for business?"

"Are you kidding?" Julia almost laughed. "My *datt* never did anything against the *Ordnung*."

William's pulse picked up a notch when he moved the bed and saw a board he hadn't noticed during their earlier search that wasn't flush with the others.

"Look at this." Using his fingers, he tried to work the board loose. "It won't budge."

"Wait a minute." She retrieved a screwdriver from Bennie's dresser.

Will pried the board loose with the screwdriver. It lifted free. The sun was setting, and they had left the oil lamps downstairs. Julianne turned on her cell phone flashlight and shined the beam into the small cubbyhole.

William reached into the opening and pulled out an envelope. Bennie's name was written on the front. He took the cell from her hand and gave her the envelope.

Looking inside, she gasped. "It's filled with money. Twenty-dollar bills. A lot of them."

"Your father's hidden stash?"

"I doubt it. Bennie was working at the grocery to make extra money for when he and Emma married. This must be the money he saved."

She clutched it to her heart and bowed her head.

William rubbed her shoulder. "Let's go, Julie. We checked the rest of the house and the outbuildings a few days ago. We would have found the evidence then."

He slipped the board into place and returned the bed to its rightful spot.

Julianne paused at the edge of her brother's room and looked back. The sadness he read in the slump of her shoulders tugged at his heart.

"Oh, Bennie," she whispered. "Someone killed *Datt*. Did he kill you, as well? Help us find the evidence so we can find the killer."

William's heart twisted with pain as he thought of his good friend. *What secrets did you hide, Bennie? If only we could learn the truth about what happened that night.*

FOURTEEN

"That bite looks inflamed and hot to the touch," Aunt Mary said when she noticed Julianne's leg the next day. "Call the doctor."

To ease her aunt's concern, Julianne phoned the clinic and left a message. Thirty minutes later, her cell rang.

"Ms. Garber, this is Cheryl calling for Dr. Norris. He sent a prescription to the pharmacy for an antibiotic. Take all the medication, and if your symptoms don't improve within forty-eight hours, he'll need to see you."

Julianne glanced at William, who had entered the kitchen. "I'll be there later today."

"What's wrong?" William asked when she disconnected.

"My leg's worse. Aunt Mary insisted I call

the clinic. Dr. Norris ordered an antibiotic that I need to pick up at the pharmacy."

"I'll go with you."

"But—" She looked out the window. "Your farm. The livestock."

"Will be fine. I'm not letting you go into town alone."

She smiled. "Thanks, William."

"We can leave now."

Julianne glanced at the wall clock. "It's almost noon. Let's wait until after lunch."

"I have a favor to ask," Aunt Mary said. "Would you mind stopping by Rachel's house and returning her cookie container. I filled it with some of the fudge I brought from home."

Julianne smiled. "It is always best to return kindness with kindness, which is what *Mamm* used to say."

Aunt Mary nodded. "Your *mamm* was a *gut* woman, Julianne."

A *gut* woman who died too young.

After lunch, Julianne and William drove to the Krause farm. Rachel was working in the garden behind the barn. Seeing the car, she dropped the hoe she was using and ran to the drive.

Before greeting them, she glanced at the barn, then back at Julia. "I did not expect to see you so soon."

"Aunt Mary wanted us to return your container and thank you for the cookies. They were delicious."

Wringing her hands, Rachel looked at the barn again and then took the plastic container from Julianne's outstretched hand.

Concerned by her friend's behavior, Julianne stepped closer. "Is something wrong, Rachel?"

"*Yah*, it is Eli." She lowered her gaze as if embarrassed by her husband. "He does not want me talking to you."

"Why would Eli feel that way?"

"I told him I saw you, and he fears I will get involved."

Julianne didn't understand. "Involved in what?"

"In what happened to your *datt* and Bennie."

"Their deaths? The sheriff ruled it was

a murder-suicide. How would that involve you?"

Rachel's eyes widened. "Eli believes it wasn't so. He knew Bennie. Not well, but he knew enough about him to know he wasn't a murderer."

"Your husband is one of the few people in town who thinks Bennie is innocent of wrongdoing."

"Other things have happened since you have been gone. It started that night, but…"

Julianne's pulse picked up a bit. "What do you mean?"

"I mean trouble in Mountain Loft. This is not something we had before." Again, she glanced at the barn. "You have heard about Amos Koenig?"

"The name sounds familiar," Julianne said.

"He was younger than your *datt*. His wife is Hannah Gingerich Koenig."

"A tall woman, four children, twin boys and two little girls?"

"*Yah.* I thought you knew her. She was with child when Amos disappeared."

"What happened?"

Rachel shrugged. "Some said he had a wandering eye and ran off with a woman, but I do not believe this to be true."

"Who spreads such gossip?" Julianne asked.

"Too many people." Rachel narrowed her gaze. "But Amos loved his family. The baby was born three months after he disappeared. Hannah did not do well. The baby fell ill and nearly died."

"Why would he leave his family?"

"No one knows or no one is willing to say. Then not six months later, Zachariah Beechy is gone." Rachel snapped her fingers. "The same way. No reason for him to leave. A father to three children and a loving husband."

She clutched the container to her chest. "It has me worried."

"About Eli?"

"About this town and what is happening. Both women struggle to support their children. Hannah moved to Willkommen and lives near her sister and brother-in-law.

Zachariah's wife, Evelyn, plans to marry again for the sake of the children. The man is older and will provide for them, but he is not Zachariah. Also she wonders if her husband is still alive."

"What does the bishop say?"

"He says little, except that after two years, her husband is not coming home, which cut Evelyn's heart, as you can imagine."

"Both men left their wives and families without any warning?"

"It is not *gut, yah*?"

"Any other missing people?"

"This is enough, for certain." She squeezed Julianne's hand. "I did not mention this when I brought the cookies. After what happened to you, I did not want to bring more bad news."

Rachel turned toward the garden and then glanced back at Julianne. "Be careful, my friend. There are secrets in Mountain Loft that no one wants uncovered."

"Amos and Zachariah are in a different church district," William said once they were in Julianne's car, heading to town. "They live farther out in the country, so I did not know about their disappearances."

"No one talks about them being gone?" she asked.

"I have not heard talk," he admitted. "But you know the Amish are not prone to spread stories."

She raised her brow and glanced at William. "Except if men have left their wives or if a double homicide is incorrectly labeled a murder-suicide. Those type of stories continue to be spread."

"The only time I have heard your father's and brother's deaths mentioned is with the *Englischers*, and then only that it was a sad situation."

"Yet husbands—like Eli Krause and Mose Miller—do not want their wives talking to me."

"Perhaps the husbands do not want their wives talking to anyone."

Julianne remained pensive until they arrived in town. She parked in front of the sheriff's office, and William accompanied her inside. Sheriff Paul Taylor invited them into his office, where they settled into the same chairs as their last visit.

"Have you found the man who attacked me?" Julianne asked, cutting to the chase.

From her tone of voice, the sheriff had to know she wasn't satisfied with his investigation. William knew it, as well, and didn't blame her. A lot had happened since she had arrived in Mountain Loft, and the sheriff didn't seem eager to find the man with the bandana or any man who might be out to do her harm.

"We captured a visual of the guy off a video camera from the bank across the street. His face was covered by that bandana you mentioned. He appears to be about six feet tall and weighs about two hundred pounds. His black tactical slacks look like police wear. Anyone can order them online. The jacket might be army surplus, or he could have been in the military."

"Which narrows it down to a lot of *Englischers*," William said.

The sheriff didn't look pleased by the

comment. "I talked to Harvey Jones to see if he'd ever sold tactical gear over the years. I also checked with Ace Reed at Reed's Dry Goods. Neither man stocks tactical gear at this time. Ace brought in the pants a few years ago, but they didn't sell fast enough, and he put them on sale."

"Does he have a record of who purchased them?"

"Not that far back. But we'll keep our eyes open."

"What about the car? Have you questioned people in town who own a white car?"

"I hate to tell you how many we found. White's a popular color, but my guys are canvasing the owners."

"Let me guess," Julianne said. "Nothing's turned up yet."

"One of the Reynolds brothers just bought a new white SUV."

William glanced at Julianne.

"You said the car that chased after you was midsize," the sheriff continued. "Any idea about the make and model?"

She shook her head. "I don't know cars, but it looked midsize and four-door."

"When I talked to you at the clinic, you mentioned the near collision with an SUV coming from the old quarry. Could the car that first night have been an SUV?"

"I'm not sure." She hesitated for a moment. "But if you suspect one of the Reynolds brothers, why would he be hanging around my farmhouse?"

"You tell me," the sheriff said.

"I don't have a clue. Nor do I know why someone would throw me into a Dumpster."

The sheriff spread his hands open on his desk. "I thought we went over that."

"You mean he wanted me to end up in the trash compactor?"

The sheriff shrugged. "The timing was right."

Julianne looked away and bit her lip.

Knowing she needed a moment to regain her composure, William mentioned another problem. "Julianne and I learned Amos Koenig and Zachariah Beechy went missing some time ago, Sheriff. Any idea of what was going on?"

Taylor steepled his fingers. "Farmers have a hard time these days. Doubt I need to tell you that, William. They're relying on Mother Nature and the Good Lord for crops to grow, and then when harvest comes, market prices drop or the buyers aren't there. Suicide's high among the farm community."

"You think they took their own lives?"

"That's one possibility."

"But no bodies were found," William persisted. "No suicide notes."

"No evidence of foul play, either," the sheriff added.

"That means three Amish men in Mountain Loft have taken their own lives within the last few years."

"Three men?" The sheriff pursed his lips.

"You claimed my brother committed suicide," Julianne reminded him.

"But that was different."

"Because you found his body?" she asked.

"It was cut-and-dried, so to speak. No question about what had happened."

She tsked. "Some don't agree with you."

"Who?"

"I'm not sharing names, but I don't see how my brother could have killed my father or himself."

"I understand, Ms. Graber. Murder and suicide are hard to accept."

She narrowed her gaze. "Did you tell that to Amos Koenig's and Zachariah Beechy's wives?"

"It's likely the men left town."

"What makes you think that?" Julianne asked.

The sheriff hesitated, as if deciding whether to share more information. "According to the wives, their husbands had kept cash on hand at their houses for any unforeseen emergencies. In both cases, the money was missing along with the men."

William glanced at Julianne. Her eyes widened. Evidently, she was thinking the same thing he was. Missing money from three Amish men. Amos, Zachariah and Julianne's *datt*. Two men were missing. One was dead.

"They could have been robbed and killed and their bodies disposed of." She frowned. "Maybe they ended up in a Dumpster and were compacted with the garbage."

The sheriff sighed. "There was no sign of a break-in at either home and no suspects, Ms. Graber. My guess is the men got tired of their lives—some call it a midlife crisis—and left everything behind."

"Including their wives and children?" Julianne countered.

"It's happened before."

The sheriff wouldn't budge from his position, but he was right. Some men made poor choices and left their families behind, searching for a better life, but it was a rare occurrence within the Amish community.

"Is there anything else?" The sheriff seemed eager for them to leave.

"Mose Miller has ridden by a number of times and seems interested in my farm."

The sheriff frowned. "Did he talk to you about buying your property?"

She shook her head. "No, but he had access to a key to my house."

"That's interesting," Sheriff Taylor rubbed his jaw.

"Mose may not have the money so he wants to scare me away," she continued. "Before long, the county would claim my property was abandoned. Mose probably thinks he could get the farm for a good price if the bank takes over the sale."

"Brad Abbott has been tasked to sell the abandoned properties. He worked that out with the mayor. Brad's got some guy from Atlanta interested in real estate around here. Sounds like he'll buy anything that goes on the market."

William didn't like the sweet deal Brad Abbott had arranged with the mayor. If Julianne listed her farm with Brad or if she vacated the property, either way the real-estate agent would still make money. William needed to learn more about Brad Abbott, and he knew someone who might provide answers.

They left the sheriff's office and headed to the grocery. Harvey waved from the hallway, where he was unloading a carton of produce when they stepped inside.

Nancy came out from behind the counter. "It's good to be see you, Julianne. When Harvey told me what happened, I feared you would be holed up at home for some time. How are you?"

"I'm doing well, and I'm very grateful for your thoughtfulness. The basket of fruit was lovely. You shouldn't have, but I greatly appreciate your kindness."

"I was upset when I heard about the attack." The older woman shivered. "Who would do such a thing and throw you into the trash receptacle?"

"Don't worry, I'm fine, but I did want to thank you personally for the fruit basket. You and Harvey have always had a special place in my heart."

"We feel the same." Seemingly pleased with the comment, Nancy opened her arms and hugged Julianne. "Tell your aunt to come to town with you one of these days, and we can have tea together."

"I know she'd enjoy seeing you."

On the way out of the store, they spotted Deputy O'Reilly. He hurried to meet them at the front of the grocery.

Harvey followed them outside and waved to the deputy. "I've got your order ready, Terry. Do you need anything else?"

"A bag of chips and a jar of salsa."

Harvey gave him a thumbs-up. "I'll get that for you."

"Thanks. I'll be there in a minute, Harvey."

"Take your time." He waved to Julianne and William. "Good seeing both of you."

O'Reilly turned to Julianne. "I saw you leaving the sheriff's office. Has anything new happened?"

"Only that the sheriff doesn't seem interested in finding the man or men who attacked me."

"We've been checking white cars registered in the area, but it's a slow go. A few vagrants have been rounded up and questioned. Nothing seems to be breaking. Did anything else happen?"

"Nothing since yesterday," William admitted. "But Mose Miller passes by every evening on his way to the lake. I'm wondering what he's doing."

"He's probably fishing."

"Which is what his wife claimed, but I wonder if he's up to something else, especially since he could have a key to the Graber home."

"That's interesting." The deputy thought for a moment and then said, "Tell you what, Will, I'm on duty tonight. I'll head down to the lake and see if I can find him. The season for night fishing doesn't open until May. Mose isn't following the regulations, which is a good reason to question him."

"Be careful," William advised. "He's not to be trusted."

"Remember to let the law handle this, Will."

"I'm not out to get Mose, but I want Julianne to remain safe."

"That's what I want, as well."

Julianne stepped closer. "That night at my house, Terry, you mentioned a deputy sheriff who had retired."

O'Reilly nodded. "Ike Vaughn."

"You said he lives in the mountains."

"He had a place in town before he retired. Then he bought the Reynolds cabin not long after Seth went to jail. It's about twenty miles from here."

"Up the mountain, along the cliff road?" Will asked.

"That's it. The drive is breathtaking in good weather, but don't go at night or if the weather is bad. I'm sure he moved up there because he was fed up with what was going on around here."

"Does Ike have a temper?" she asked.

The deputy raised his brow. "Meaning what?"

"You said he butted heads with the sheriff."

"A lot of folks do, but Ike held his ground. Then turned in his resignation."

O'Reilly glanced at the distant clouds. "If you're heading to Ike's place, my suggestion is to go now. Bad weather's coming in tonight. I wouldn't want you stuck on the mountain."

William didn't want that, either.

On the way to Julianne's car, he grabbed her arm. "Wait up a minute." Nodding toward the opposite side of the street, he stopped.

Julianne followed his gaze. "Is that Ralph Reynolds, talking to someone in a buggy?" she asked.

"That's not someone. That's Mose Miller."

Ralph was waving his arms and seemed to be in a heated discussion with Mose.

"Ralph doesn't look happy," Julianne said.

"That's an understatement. Wonder what's going on between them?"

Ralph turned away from Mose abruptly, climbed into his car and drove away. Mose glanced around as if to ensure the argument hadn't been seen. Noticing William and Julianne, he narrowed his gaze and stared at them.

"He gives me the heebie-jeebies," Julianne admitted as they climbed into her car.

"I'd like to make a stop after the pharmacy."

"You want to talk to Gloria?" Julianne asked.

"How did you know?"

She smiled. "You were eager to talk to her the last time we were in town, I thought something had started between you two again."

"That's absurd, but I do want to question her about Ralph."

"I doubt Ralph would want you talking to his girlfriend, especially if he *is* the subject of the discussion."

She pulled into a parking spot in front of the real-estate office. "The pharmacy is across the street. I'll pick up my prescription while you're with Gloria."

"We'll go together, and after you purchase the meds, you can lock yourself in your car while I talk to Gloria."

Julie laughed. "Aren't you being a little overprotective?"

"Maybe, but that's a good thing."

She smiled. "You're right, Will, and I appreciate your concern."

Once she had the antibiotic and a bottle of water, she took the first pill and hurried back to her car to wait for him.

William gave her a thumbs-up before

he entered the real-estate office and then groaned when he didn't see Gloria. Before he could retreat outside, he heard her call his name.

"I didn't expect to see you today." She came out of Brad Abbott's office and closed the door behind her. "Did you change your mind about what we talked about the other day?"

"Gloria, did Ralph ask you to distract me so I wouldn't be with Julianne?"

"What do you mean?"

"Did he tell you to talk to me so Julie would be on her own? That would give Ralph an opportunity to grab her and throw her in the garbage receptacle."

"I heard what happened, but Ralph would never do something like that. Plus, he wasn't in town that day."

"Are you sure?"

"He was with his younger brother."

"You mean Seth?"

She nodded. "He's out of jail and trying to get his life clean. Ralph's been helping him."

"Seth must be doing something right. I heard he's driving a new car."

"Ralph says he has his hands in a lot of ventures."

"Business deals?" Will asked.

She shrugged. "I'm not sure."

"What about your boss? Is he on the up-and-up?"

"Did Julianne tell you to ask me about Brad?"

"I'm asking. This deal he has with the mayor to sell abandoned property sounds a little too sweet."

"Then maybe you should discuss it with the mayor." She huffed.

"What about Mose Miller? Ralph's involved with him in some way. What do you know about that?"

She glanced down and started rearranging the papers on her desk.

"You know something, Gloria." He stepped closer. "What's going on?"

She shook her head. "You'll have to ask Ralph. I don't know anything about Mose

Miller except that he and Emma are going to have a baby."

"Is it about buying land? Or scaring folks off their property so Brad can sell the land at a lower price?"

"That's absurd." She glanced at her boss's office. "I need to get back to work, William. Thanks for stopping by."

The phone rang. She lifted the receiver to her ear and glared at him as if willing him to leave.

He'd leave, but he knew she wasn't telling the truth. Something was going on between Ralph and Mose. He didn't trust either of them. Brad Abbott could be involved, too.

William hurried outside, but his heart stopped when he looked at the parking spot where he'd left Julianne.

Her car was gone, and so was she.

FIFTEEN

Julianne placed the gas nozzle back in the pump, relieved she had looked at her car's fuel gauge. If she and William had headed up the mountain with a near empty tank of gas, they could have ended up stranded on the side of the road.

She rounded her car to climb behind the wheel when she saw Emma Miller come out of the fabric shop. Hurrying toward her, she waved her hand. "Emma."

The Amish woman turned and started to smile, then glanced down the road before she crossed the street, carrying her shopping bag.

"Julianne, I heard you had been injured. What is happening?"

"That's what I'm trying to find out."

"You are all right?"

"A little bruised and confused about why someone wants me gone." She stared at Emma. "Would Mose try to scare me away?"

"Of course not. Mose has a temper, this is true, but he is not a wicked man."

"I didn't say he was. What about the key to my house, Emma? Did you find it?"

"Not yet."

"You mentioned evidence Bennie had collected. I searched but could find nothing at the house. Do you know where he hid the information?"

A buggy sounded behind them. Emma glanced over her shoulder, a worried look on her face. She squeezed Julianne's hand. "Get into your car and drive away now. Mose must not see you."

Emma hurried back toward the fabric shop.

Mose drew his buggy to a stop, hopped out and then grabbed his wife's arm and shoved her toward the rig. Julianne's heart broke seeing the way he treated Emma.

She started across the street. "Stop it, Mose. You're hurting Emma. Let go of her."

He snarled, shoved Emma into the buggy and climbed in next to her.

Julianne moved closer. "Emma, you don't have to settle for that kind of treatment. Let me help you."

Her friend shook her head. Fear flashed from her eyes.

Julianne had made the situation worse, when all she'd wanted was to help Emma.

Mose grabbed the whip and applied it to the mare. The horse took off at a fast clip, heading right for Julianne. Emma screamed and tried to grab the reins. He shoved her aside, flicked the reins and urged the mare to go even faster.

Julianne jumped back just before the buggy raced past her.

Emma stared at Julianne and mouthed something.

Julianne shook her head, trying to let Emma know she couldn't understand what her friend was trying to tell her.

Emma glanced at her husband and then

back at Julianne. She pretended to pull something from the waistband of her dress and press it to her ear. A phone. A cell phone.

Emma was telling Julianne where Bennie might have hidden the evidence. On his cell phone.

William was overcome with dread as Mose raced his buggy down the street, going much too fast. Instinctively, Will knew Julianne had been involved. He ran to the intersection and stared in the direction from which the buggy had just come.

Julianne stood on the side of road.

"What happened?" he asked as he hurried toward her.

"Mose is a twisted man, which makes me all the more concerned about Emma." Julianne quickly explained what had happened. "I shouldn't have called out to him, but I didn't want Emma to get hurt."

"You tried to help. That's not a bad thing."

"There has to be someone Mose would

listen to. The bishop or one of the other preachers, perhaps?"

"Growing up, Mose had seemed to admire Deacon Abe Schwartz. His farm is on the mountain road. We'll pass it on our way to Ike Vaughn's cabin."

"Deacon Schwartz will probably ignore me, but let's stop, anyway. You might be able to convince him to talk to Mose. Someone has to."

Abe owned a considerable amount of land. He was training a horse in the paddock when Julianne pulled the car to a stop not far from the house. Abe scowled at her as she climbed from the car, then turned his back and continued to work with the young filly.

"I told you he wouldn't want to see me."

William recognized the pain in Julianne's voice.

Mrs. Schwartz stepped onto the porch and wiped her hands on a dish towel. "Why, Julianne Graber, I heard you had come home to Mountain Loft. We've missed you."

The words of welcome brought a smile to

Julianne's lips. "William wanted to talk to Deacon Schwartz for a few minutes."

"Good to see you, Will." Mrs. Schwartz motioned him forward. "Go to the paddock. Abe will talk to you there."

Abe stopped working with the filly as Will neared the gate to the paddock. The deacon glanced at where Julianne and his wife chatted. "I hope you have not come to tell me your heart has taken over your head. Julianne Graber is a pretty woman, and had she remained Amish, I could see you together, but she has abandoned her past. Her mistake should not be yours."

Surprised that the deacon thought he was leaving his faith behind, William was quick to reassure him. "I have no intention of leaving the faith, Deacon Schwartz. I am a better man living within the community, but there is another matter I want to discuss with you."

He explained what he had observed concerning Mose and his wife. "He could use your counsel."

Abe nodded and rubbed his beard. "I

am going to town today and will stop on the way to talk to the bishop. You are not the first to mention a concern. I am disappointed Mose's father has not addressed the problem."

"Either he looks the other way," William said, "or it's more likely Mose has closed his ears to his father's advice."

Abe nodded. "As we both know, life can get complicated when one strays from the dictates of *Gott*."

William was grateful he had seen the errors of his own youthful ways. He hoped Mose would, as well.

Whether the deacon talked to him or not, Mose Miller was trouble, and William needed to ensure he never had an opportunity to hurt Julianne again.

The mountain road was worse than the drive from Dahlonega, and Julianne's hands ached from her tight grip on the steering wheel. She hugged the mountain and tried not to glance over the drop-off on the far side of the narrow two-lane road.

"Why would the deputy move up here?" she asked. "Having to drive along such a treacherous roadway would make me a nervous wreck."

"From what Terry said, Ike was fed up with the sheriff. He probably wanted to distance himself from people in town, as well." William pointed to the bend in the road. "His cabin should be on the other side of the bend. I've been up here before."

"Were you friends with Seth Reynolds?"

"For a short period of time. I knew one of Seth's uncles, the one who owned the cabin initially. Ralph lived with him for a while before Seth got into trouble with the law."

"You know everyone."

William chuckled. "I should have done a better job picking the people with whom I associated in my youth. I'm thankful Seth's antics didn't rub off on me and grateful I found other people to call my friends."

"Like Bennie."

Will nodded. "Bennie and I were more like brothers, growing up on neighboring farms. He was a good influence and had a better head on his shoulders than I did in my teen years."

"Bennie knew what he wanted and what was important. He had his life planned out, and he was making his dreams come true. Until…"

William rubbed her arm as they rounded the bend. The small cabin stood on a rise.

"Turn onto the dirt road and stop some distance from the house. I don't want Ike to think we're up to no good."

Julianne pulled onto the dirt drive and parked.

"Perfect," William said. "He'll be able to see us from here and realize we're friends and not foes."

"You're making me afraid of meeting Deputy Vaughn."

"He suggested I leave Mountain Loft after Bennie and your *datt* died."

"Suggested as in ordered you to leave?"

"Hardly. He advised me like a father would. Told me people would talk because Bennie and I were close. With my penchant for getting into scrapes, he said I would be the likely target when folks were looking for someone to blame."

"And you believed him?"

He shrugged. "I knew how people talked, and some folks turned up their noses when I walked by them."

"Like the way Deacon Schwartz treated me."

"You understand how that feels."

She nodded. "And I don't blame you for leaving."

"At that time, my *datt* and I couldn't see eye to eye on anything, so it seemed like the best thing to do. Later, I realized I was being cowardly. It's a better man who stays instead of running away."

"Then you can call me a coward." She sighed. "I ran away and never planned to come back."

"But you're here now, which is all that matters." His smile warmed her heart as he grabbed the door handle. "I'll see if I can locate Ike."

"After that killer drive, I'll be disappointed if we don't find him."

William stepped from the car, closed the door with a slam and waited to see if he got a response. The door to the cabin remained closed.

Julianne was worried. The last thing she wanted was to surprise the deputy.

Heart pounding at a rapid pace, she stepped out of the car and kept her gaze on the wooded area surrounding the cabin. Julianne didn't like surprises, especially from a man who might not want visitors encroaching on his property and his privacy.

SIXTEEN

Julianne continued to stare at the wooded area and the path that ran around the rear of the house. William cupped his hand around his mouth and called the deputy's name.

"It's William Lavy, sir. I need to talk to you."

The barrel of a rifle appeared at the corner of the small barn. A man stepped into view. He looked to be in his sixties and had gray hair and a full beard.

He glared at both of them. "You're trespassing on private property so state your business and don't give me any guff."

"Sir, remember me? I'm William Lavy from Mountain Loft. You reached out to me a number of times when I was a teen. I appreciated your advice, even if I did not always comply with your directives."

The older man narrowed his gaze. "Your daddy was Benjamin Lavy?"

Will nodded. "My family lived on the road to the lake near the Grabers." He pointed to Julie. "This is Daniel Graber's daughter, Julianne."

Ike stared at her. "You look like your mother."

She smiled at the compliment. "I need to talk to you about my father's and brother's deaths."

He glanced around them at the car. "Anyone else with you?"

William shook his head. "No, sir. Deputy Terence O'Reilly told us you didn't side with Sheriff Taylor when it came to the Graber investigation."

"What investigation? Paul Taylor took the easy way out." As Julianne watched, Ike set his jaw in frustration and then pointed to the Adirondack chairs on the porch. "Have a seat. We can talk out here and enjoy the fresh air."

"As you know all too well, Mr. Vaughn," Julianne began once they had settled into the chairs, "Sheriff Paul Taylor decided, following a rather brief criminal investigation, that my brother, Bennie, argued with my father, shot him and then turned the gun on himself in what the sheriff claimed was a murder-suicide. I wanted to get your opinion. You were there that morning."

Ike rubbed his beard. "The call came while I was on duty, although I can't remember who contacted Dispatch."

"My *datt* ran to a neighbor's phone shack and called the sheriff's office," Will explained. "I stayed with Julianne."

The former deputy nodded. "I was in my patrol car, hit the lights and siren and got out there fast as I could." He glanced at Julianne. "I'm not sure how much you remember, girlie, but it was the worst crime we've had in this town."

"Did the sheriff arrive soon after you?" she asked.

"Took him a bit of time, but he got there. I taped off the area, took photos on my phone and searched the yard for evidence."

"Did you find anything?"

He shook his head. "Nothing in the yard."

"What about inside the house?"

"Daniel Graber was on the floor at the foot of the stairs with a gunshot wound to his chest."

"And my brother, Bennie?"

"That's the strange part. He's sitting there with his back against the wall, shot in the chest, but he was still clutching his weapon."

William scooted closer. "He should have dropped the gun?"

Ike shrugged. "That's hard to say, but there was blood spatter higher on the wall."

"So he shot himself when he was standing," William said. "That makes sense, right?"

"Except he slipped down into a perfect sitting position and died there. A little too nice and neat if you ask me. Plus, as I said, his fingers were still curled around the weapon."

Julianne rubbed her hand over her temple, trying to remove the image that seemed too real.

"What about fingerprints on the weapon?" Will asked.

"We only found Bennie's prints, but the gun could have been wiped clean and then placed in his hand." Ike paused for a moment. "When men take their own lives with a handgun, they don't want to survive." He glanced at Julianne. "I hate to upset you, ma'am, but they usually aim at their heads."

She grimaced.

"One more thing." Ike held up two fingers. "There were two bullets and two shell casings. Sheriff Taylor should have sent them off for a ballistics check. Pretty basic protocol for a death investigation, only he presumed they came from the same weapon, namely Bennie's nine-millimeter Smith & Wesson."

"The gun my brother was holding belonged to him?"

Ike nodded. "He had purchased the weapon two weeks earlier from a dealer in Willkommen, but I can't say for sure that either man was killed by Bennie's Smith & Wesson."

"I saw my father on the floor when I came home that night, then someone behind me said my name." She raked her hand through her hair. "At least, I think it was my name. Before I could turn around, something struck me on the head."

"Did you think it was your brother?" he asked.

"I wasn't thinking, but if someone else killed my father, wouldn't they have also killed me?"

She shared what her brother's former girl-friend had told them about Bennie meeting with a man involved in some type of illegal operation. "At that time, Ike, did you suspect anything underhanded was going on in town?"

The retired deputy shrugged. "A lot can happen when people are greedy for money and power. I thought the sheriff was a little too tight with the mayor and listened to his counsel more than I would have liked." He glanced at Will. "That's why I suggested you leave town for a while after the murders. Out of sight, out of mind, if you know what I mean. People were eager to jump to conclusions, and I knew you weren't involved."

"I'm grateful for your support."

Ike chuckled. "That's not to say you were a model kid, Will, but your heart was in the right place. Plus, I knew your dad. He didn't give anyone the benefit of the doubt. Hard to live up to his standards, I'm sure."

"We reconciled after he got sick. I was able to forgive him, and he forgave me. That healed a lot of past pain."

Julianne could feel William's gaze.

"Sometimes we hang on to baggage that needs to be tossed down the mountain," he added.

The deputy nodded. "I retired because I was angry about how justice was carried out in town. Living up here..." He glanced around the property. "Living here puts everything in perspective. I had to let the past go."

"You bought this cabin from the Reynolds family," William said. "Seth is out of jail now and driving a new SUV, from what I've heard."

Ike whistled. "The sheriff needs to check

out where he's getting his money. Truth is, I bought the cabin from Seth's uncle. He's not much better than his nephew. I'm convinced he's got a still near the creek, but I haven't found it yet."

"He's making moonshine?"

"That's right, and selling it to some of the mountain men. Seth might be working for him, but I doubt he could afford an SUV, no matter how much moonshine he sells."

Ike sat back and shared stories about the mountain men who had caused problems over the years. His tales were spiced with humor that made Julianne laugh.

"I've talked too long," Ike finally said, although his eyes twinkled and a smile covered his wide face.

"Thank you for the information about that night," Julianne said as she rose from the chair.

"Anytime. You know where to find me." He shook William's hand. "I've delayed your trip back to town with my stories."

"Not a problem. It's been good to see you again, sir."

"Safe trip to both of you."

The sun hung low in the sky, and Julianne worried about the encroaching darkness. She was tired when they got on the road, but her mind was working overtime. "If Bennie didn't kill my dad, then who did?"

"Probably the guy with the illegal business deal."

She nodded. "Which means we have to find the evidence that Bennie tried to hide. That way, we'll know who killed him. My *datt* probably heard Bennie and the man arguing. When he came downstairs, the guy shot him."

"Then he killed Bennie and staged his body to look like he had taken his own life. He could've gone outside and discharged a couple rounds with Bennie's gun so law enforcement could tell it had been fired. Then he wiped it clean and wrapped Bennie's hand around the weapon. You and I were still at the lake, Julie, so we didn't hear the gunfire, and my father was a sound sleeper."

"I keep wondering why the murderer didn't kill me?"

"Maybe because he knew Bennie wouldn't

have killed you. You never saw him, Julianne, so he thought he could escape without notice."

"Except his car passed Rachel while she was hiding in the woods."

"If that was the killer, then we know he drives a white car."

"Which seems to be popular in Mountain Loft. But that was five years ago. He could have sold it by now."

The road narrowed even more, and the outer edge disappeared over the steep drop-off. Julianne stopped talking to devote all of her attention to the road.

"You're doing a *gut* job," William assured her.

"Did I tell you that I don't like heights?"

"You could pull off the road and let me drive if you'd feel better." He glanced out the side window. "Although I don't know where you'd pull over."

"Just as long as a car doesn't approach us from the other way. Even worse would be a large van or a truck as narrow as this road is."

Rain started to fall, which made a bad situation even worse. She flicked on the windshield wipers and headlights and leaned closer to the window in order to see through the fat drops that increased in intensity.

"Not much longer," William assured her. "We're almost at the bottom of this steep section of the mountain."

William's voice was calming, but she didn't feel his optimism. Her mouth was dry, and her ears roared over the now-pounding rain.

She kept her foot on the brake and hoped the tires would continue to grip the road as the pouring rain washed across the pavement.

Julianne tapped the brake and felt the wheels skid. Her pulse raced. She turned into the skid, ever so slightly. If she overcorrected too much, they'd be hurled off the side of the mountain.

A curve appeared ahead. Her heart nearly pounded out of her chest. She inched around the bend, anticipating an approaching vehicle, and let out a sigh of relief when she saw no one was heading up the mountain.

A loud rumble sounded overhead.

William glanced up through the front window and gasped.

"Hit the brakes. Now!"

She pushed on the brake pedal. The back wheels skidded, and the car fishtailed toward the edge. Her heart lodged in her throat. She clutched the wheel and turned into the skid.

Gravel rained down on her car. The roar grew louder and closer. She pumped the brake and held her breath as a giant boulder bounced across the road, clipped the hood of her car and plunged over the cliff.

The jolt to the car caused her head to slam against the seat, but she kept her grip on the steering wheel and her foot on the brake. "Please, *Gott*!"

The car turned sideways and started to skid down the steep incline. She turned the wheel and gasped with relief when they angled back onto the roadway.

"Keep it steady," William cautioned. "You're doing fine."

"I can't."

"You can. Don't think about the rock. We're almost to the plateau. Just a little farther."

Warning lights flashed on the dashboard. "The engine temperature is rising. What should I do?"

"Pull over to the side of the road as soon as you can."

"But where?"

"We'll get to the plateau in a minute or so."

Not soon enough.

She glanced at her rearview mirror. Headlights appeared behind them.

"Someone's approaching."

"Turn on your hazard lights so the driver sees you."

She hit the button on her dash, and the lights blinked.

The car was getting closer. "Why doesn't he slow down?"

William glanced back. "He's got to see us."

"Maybe he doesn't want to stop."

The car was on her tail, then drew closer and tapped her rear bumper. Her car jerked forward.

The car accelerated and hit the rear bumper again.

Julianne's hands ached, but she continued

to hold the wheel. The gauges flashed. They wouldn't make it down the mountain alive.

"We're almost to the plateau," Will said.

But the guy would run them off the road before they got there. The road widened, and a clearing appeared on the right. A car sat parked in the small turnaround area. Julianne gasped with relief when she recognized the sheriff's car.

Sheriff Taylor rolled down his window when she pulled up next to him. "You folks got a problem?"

"Go after that car." Julianne pointed to the white vehicle that raced past the clearing. "The driver tried to run us off the road."

The sheriff grabbed his radio and called Dispatch. "Tell O'Reilly to follow a midsize SUV, color white, heading into town on the mountain road. Have him pull the driver over and call me."

As the sheriff continued to issue orders to his dispatcher, Julianne turned to William. All the tension that had built up during their ride down the mountain swelled up within her.

"I thought..." She gasped for air. "I thought we'd go off the road and over the cliff."

He reached for her and pulled her into his arms. She closed her eyes and listened to the pounding of his heart, drawing strength from him.

"You did it, Julianne. You drove us down the mountain."

"How...?" She pulled back ever so slightly. "How did the boulder break free?"

"Rockslides happen, but I think someone pushed that particular rock free."

"And then the same person tried to run us off the road."

"Either way, he wanted you to lose control of the car."

"And if that had happened," Julianne said, "we would have been hurled over the side of the mountain."

"Don't think of what could have happened," William offered.

But that's all Julianne could think about, knowing that the man wouldn't give up until she was dead.

* * *

A tow truck from Smithy's Garage hauled Julianne's car to town. The mechanic on duty quickly assessed the problem and met them outside on the garage driveway.

"I'll need a couple days to work on your car," he explained. "The boulder cracked the radiator. Water spewed out and the temperature rose. Your engine would have burned up if you had driven much farther. Good thing you pulled over at the clearing."

"Good thing the sheriff was parked there," William told Julianne when the mechanic returned to his work. "Or no telling what the driver would have done. The sheriff said it was an SUV, but the car passed too quickly for him to identify the make or model."

Deputy O'Reilly pulled to a stop in front of the garage, rolled down his patrol car window and called to them. "I heard what happened. Sounds like a close call."

"At least we made it off the mountain alive," Will said.

"Did you apprehend the driver of the SUV?" Julianne asked.

"I checked out the lake and found Mose Miller."

Evidently the deputy hadn't heard her question about the SUV.

She and Will stepped closer to the roadway. "Was Mose fishing?"

"Hardly. He was minding a still."

"Moonshine?" Will asked.

"He mentioned working for Seth Reynolds."

"Ralph's brother?"

"That's right. He got out of jail not long ago and seems to have gone into a lot of business endeavors, none of them legal. Rumor has it he runs a still near one of the mountain creeks, although I've never been able to find it. Seems he branched out with a second still near the lake that Mose manages at night."

"Ike suspected the uncle was making moonshine," Will revealed. "Sounds like a family operation."

"An operation that included a new hire. Namely Mose Miller, although considering the way I found him today, he might be drinking most of the profits. He's sleeping

it off in jail tonight. The sheriff will inter-
rogate him tomorrow."

"Let us know if he confesses to attacking
me," Julianne said.

"I'm sure he'll have a lot to share tomorrow. His hands and arms were scratched.
He claims he fell into a blackberry bush,
but the cuts look like fingernail gashes to
me. Also, he delivers his hooch to customers
using Seth's SUV, which was parked near
the still. We'll hold him for as long as we
can and see what he has to reveal. Justice
can move slowly in a small town. Knowing
the way Sheriff Taylor operates, Mose could
be off the streets for quite a few days."

"I'm relieved," William said. Although if
Seth's SUV was the car that tried to drive
them off the mountain road, how had Mose
maneuvered the vehicle down the treacherous road if he had been drinking?

"Did you follow the SUV to the still?"
William asked.

The deputy looked confused.

"The sheriff called the dispatcher," William explained. "He wanted you to appre-

hend the driver who tried to run us off the mountain road."

"I never got the message. Reception is bad at the lake. I was dealing with Mose at the time."

"Did the sheriff know where you were?"

"Of course."

But he had led William and Julianne to believe O'Reilly would chase down the driver of the white SUV.

"You folks need a ride home?" O'Reilly asked.

"I already called the Amish taxi. It'll be here in about five minutes."

"Sorry about the car," O'Reilly said. "But I'm glad you weren't hurt."

William was relieved they were both alive, but he was concerned about the sheriff and whether he could be trusted. Or was he keeping secrets like so many people seemed to be doing in Mountain Loft?

SEVENTEEN

Aunt Mary met William and Julianne at the door when they returned to his house and listened as they shared what had happened.

"Ack," the older woman lamented. "You both could have been killed by the boulder—then to have someone try to run you off the road. Remember that Anna Jones died in an automobile crash on the mountain. It can happen even when we are careful."

"I'm grateful William told me to brake," Julianne said.

"And I'm glad you responded so quickly," he added. "A second or two longer, and things could have turned out differently."

Aunt Mary patted her chest. "Do not mention what could have happened. We must focus on the fact you weren't hurt. It is because of *Gott*'s mercy." She glanced at Julianne. "The Lord spared you for a reason."

From the tightness of her brow, Julie appeared unsure about who had saved her. She sat at the table and looked exhausted. William sat across from Julianne and explained to her aunt what Ike Vaughn had told them.

After pouring coffee, Aunt Mary brought the filled cups to the table. "I'm glad the former deputy believes Bennie is innocent of wrongdoing."

"I am, as well," Julianne agreed. "But that means the killer is still on the loose, and if so, he's probably the man with the bandana." She sighed. "I don't know why he wants me dead."

"Perhaps he thinks you know something, dear."

"Or does he fear you will uncover the missing evidence that Bennie gathered before his death?" William mused.

Julianne sipped the coffee. "Which leads me to believe the evidence must be at my house."

"Tomorrow we will search again," Aunt

Mary suggested. "But now I must tell you what I learned when the mailman delivered the mail today. We chatted for a few minutes, and he shared the news."

"From the look on your face, Aunt Mary, the news must not be good."

"Another tragedy. This time it is a friend of your father's, Julianne. He was crossing a stream behind his farm. The water was high due to the storms. Somehow, he slipped off the small bridge and hit his head when he was thrown into the water. His body was found farther downstream."

"A friend of *Datt*'s?"

"Deacon Abraham Schwartz."

Julianne gasped. "We were with him this afternoon. He has a wife and children."

"Five children." Aunt Mary nodded. "The youngest is four years old. The funeral is day after tomorrow. I will go." She glanced at William. "You will go with me?"

"For certain."

"I'll join you," Julianne said. "He was *Datt*'s friend. I need to be there. Deacon

Schwartz may have turned his back on me, but I will not turn my back on his family."

Julianne found the black Amish dress she had worn to her father's and brother's burials packed away in a chest at her house, as well as a blue dress and another black dress that would fit her aunt. The morning of the funeral, William—also dressed in black—helped them climb into the buggy.

The air was somber as they traveled toward the Schwartz farm. The morning chill and the rhythmic clip-clop of the horse's hooves on the pavement brought back memories that weighed heavily on Julianne's heart. Along the way, they were joined by other Amish buggies, and she recognized many people she had known in her youth.

As William guided his mare onto the Schwartz property, her chest constricted. Clutching her hands together on her lap, she wondered if she had made a mistake in coming to bid farewell to the deceased deacon.

The mourners were subdued as they left

their buggies and headed to the barn. A few people averted their gazes when Julianne stepped into the area cleared for the occasion. Unwilling to dwell on their rejection, she squared her shoulders and held her head high. Non-Amish were allowed to attend funerals. Not even the bishop would call her to task.

Wooden benches were arranged on either side of the pine coffin. The men sat together, across from the women. The bishop and two other ministers took their places in front of the men. The bishop talked of the creation story with emphasis on the teaching that man had been created from dust and would return to dust at the end of life.

Aunt Mary, her eyes lowered in prayer, sat ramrod straight on the bench next to Julianne. Turning her gaze from her aunt, she glanced at William. His cheeks were ruddy, and his eyes crystal-blue as he stared back at her. A warmth curled around her neck. His lips turned up ever so slightly into the merest hint of a smile, before he glanced back at the bishop standing near the coffin.

Julia looked down, fearing her own cheeks were flushed from the intensity of William's gaze. If anyone saw her reaction to his perusal, they would think her more interested in William than in her prayers.

Not that she cared what others thought, although in reality, she did care. She cared that they thought Bennie was a murderer. She cared that they thought she had turned *fancy* and wasn't deserving of their attention. She cared that she no longer had a community that would reach out and embrace her.

For seventeen years, she had accepted the precepts of the Amish way of life, but all that had changed, seemingly in the blink of an eye. Had she been wrong to leave her faith?

The bishop's words, spoken in the Pennsylvania Dutch language she knew so well, brought back memories of when her *mamm* and *datt* were alive, when she and Bennie were growing up and their family had been filled with love. Now, she was the only one

left, except for Aunt Mary. How had everything changed so completely?

Feeling William's gaze, she glanced up
to find him staring at her again. His eyes
were filled with understanding, as if he
could read the questions running through
her mind. His earlier hint of a smile had
been replaced with an expression that made
her heart lurch and her pulse race.

Amish and *Englisch* didn't mix, her voice
of reason warned, no matter how much she
cared for William. The only way they could
have a future together would be if she em-
braced the Amish faith, which, at the present time, she couldn't do.

Surrounded by the rituals that had given
meaning to everything in her childhood and
youth, she was overcome with sorrow and
kept her eyes downcast for the remainder of
the service. After its conclusion, the pallbearers carried the coffin to the buggy that
would transport Deacon Schwartz's remains
to his grave site. Julianne leaned against
William for support as Aunt Mary settled
into the rear seat of his buggy. He helped

Julie into the front, and she sat next to him, sensing his unease. Was he struggling, just as she was, with issues of faith?

William flicked the reins and guided his mare into the line of buggies that traveled along the country road. The rhythmic cadence of the horses' hooves was like the drumbeat of a funeral dirge, and was accompanied by the creaking of the wheels and the lament of the wind that rustled through the branches of the trees.

The mourners caravanned toward the cemetery where they would be burying a man they had held in esteem. Julianne's heart ached for the community she had known and loved, for the Schwartz family who grieved and for her own loss that still broke her heart.

William kept his gaze on the road ahead. She wanted to touch his shoulder and find some tenderness in his expression, but she saw only the tension in his neck and the thump of a heartbeat that pulsed along his temple.

Once at the cemetery, the bishop opened

the graveside service with a prayer. At the conclusion, the pallbearers lowered the hand-hewn coffin into the grave.

The end of another life. The bishop had said death was part of the life process, but so many in their community had died in tragic ways. Julianne saw the women whose husbands had disappeared. Were the men dead, or had they run off, as the sheriff suspected?

What was happening in this small Amish community? Death and grief ran rampant. Julianne couldn't take more pain. Coming home had been a mistake. She needed to leave. But she didn't want to leave without William.

After dinner that night, William went outside to check on the livestock. He also wanted to walk around his property and ensure no one was hovering in the shadows.

The day had been difficult, especially the burial. Aunt Mary had felt it would be best to return home from the grave site, so they had not joined the community back at the Schwartz farm.

Julianne had seemed unsettled at the cemetery, no doubt remembering her brother's and father's burials. Plus, William had noted the less-than-gracious welcome from some of the Amish. He had expected them to be more accepting of Julianne, since she wasn't baptized, but she had left the faith, which was the bottom line. Although she had dressed Amish, many of the more conservative members of the district could not overlook her rejection of the Amish way.

She appeared tired when they got home, and Aunt Mary insisted she rest until dinner. Julie had retired to the guest room for an hour and had reappeared to help with the meal.

"Care for a cup of coffee?"

William was in the barnyard and turned at the sound of Julianne's voice. She was still wearing the Amish dress that hung on her slender shoulders and cupped in around her waist. He couldn't help but notice the way the skirt flowed around her legs and moved with her as she descended the porch steps and met him near the water pump.

He took the cup she offered. "The night is cool, and the coffee smells *gut*. Thank you for thinking of me."

"I came outside hoping to see the stars twinkle in the night sky."

He glanced up and pointed to the Big Dipper and the North Star. "It is *gut* to see the grandeur of the sky, *yah*? It makes me appreciate *Gott*'s goodness. The entire universe comes under His care, yet He still watches over me and my needs."

"At one time I was sure of His benevolence, now..."

She glanced down and sipped from her own cup.

"You blame *Gott* for what happened?"

"I blame myself. *Gott* had nothing to do with it." She hesitated and looked at him, her eyes wide. "Although sometimes I question why He allowed it to happen, and why my father and brother both had to die. At least Ike doesn't think Bennie killed my *datt*. That is why I struggle with the sheriff."

"So where's the evidence? That's what needs to be found."

"Tomorrow, we should search the house again," she suggested.

He put his mug down near the pump and stepped closer. "I keep thinking of that night at the lake with you."

Placing her mug next to his, she smiled. "It is a *gut* memory, before the darkness that followed too soon after."

William stepped closer. "I thought we had made a connection. Talking to you was *gut*. We sat on the log by the bonfire and sang songs."

She nodded. "It was nice being together."

"Yet you said at the Country Kitchen you had wanted to keep me from Bennie. Were you tricking me that night, Julianne?"

"Oh, Will." Confusion filled her gaze as she looked up at him. "I did not tell you everything."

He waited, focused on her sweet lips and the way the starlight played over her cheeks. It took all his effort not to lift his hand to touch her hair.

She lowered her eyes for a moment before glancing up at him again. The openness of her gaze made his chest hitch.

"I went to the lake planning to deter you from following after Bennie. He drove Emma home earlier than I expected, and when you did not follow after them, I must admit to being relieved. But—"

"But what?" He moved closer and rubbed his hand over her shoulder.

"But then I forgot about Bennie and thought only of you and how your smile warmed my heart, and how your laugh was like a gentle spring breeze that made me happy. I realized you were a *gut* person, and what I had heard about you in town was wrong. I realized *Datt* was wrong about you, as well. In fact, I had planned to tell him that he needed to see you with eyes of truth instead of eyes of rumor and innuendo." She shrugged slightly. "Of course, I did not get that chance."

"I had noticed you earlier that year in a new way." He thought for a moment, trying to form his words so she would understand.

"You walked out of the house when I was with Bennie, and for the first time, I noticed the way the sunlight danced over your auburn hair, and how your face was filled with eager expectation as if you wanted to grasp every moment and live life to the fullest."

"The day you and Bennie were going to help the Widow Highbush with her plowing?"

He nodded. "You caught my gaze, and I could feel a current run through my body. You felt it, too?"

"A current is not what I would call it, but *yah*." She smiled. "Something happened when I glanced at you. Something inside me, as if a closed portion of my heart opened. After my mother died, I felt alone. *Datt* had a hard time. I—I thought he blamed me."

"Why did you think that?"

"I had been sick. My *mamm* became ill a few days later." She looked at him with tears in her eyes. "I know he blamed me."

"And what of you, Julianne?"

She raised an eyebrow. "What do you mean?"

"Did you blame yourself, as well? You believe you were responsible for your father and brother arguing and carry guilt for their deaths. Now you tell me you carry the guilt of your mother's death. Yet death is part of our human existence. Life and death are the natural way. You heard Ike say Bennie did not kill your *datt*. They were not the ones arguing. It was Bennie arguing with the man who wanted him to go into business with him. That's who is responsible."

"If what the deputy said is true."

"Your mother could have gotten sick just as you did, but not necessarily because of you. And even if she had contracted the illness from you, you did not want your mother to become ill. You are not to blame, Julianne."

She smiled weakly. "Hearing your reasoning makes me look at what happened differently. Thank you, William."

"You must listen to my words and not to the negative voice that tries to weigh you down. You are a beautiful woman, Julianne. You carry a light that brightens my world."

Her gaze pierced his heart.

"Oh, William," she whispered.

He was swept up in her allure and the warmth he saw in her eyes. Stepping closer, he wrapped her in his arms and pulled her close. He breathed in her goodness, knowing he might lose his heart at any moment.

"Julie, I..."

She lifted her lips to his, and the night stood still. All he could think of was his overwhelming wish to kiss Julianne.

Before his lips touched hers, the kitchen door opened.

"Julianne, it's cold outside." Aunt Mary stepped onto the porch. "You and William should come into the house."

Julianne pulled back. Her cheeks pinkened, and she glanced at him with sadness before she grabbed her mug and hurried inside, leaving him to stare after her.

A longing overtook him. He wanted to run after Julie and tell her the effect she had on him. Without a shadow of a doubt, he was a better man when she was in his arms.

"Are you coming in, William?" her aunt asked.

"First, I must check the barn."

William needed a long moment to still his racing heart and to focus on life as it was, and not what he wished it would be with Julianne. She would leave Mountain Loft and return to her *fancy* life.

Where would that leave him?

Alone and despondent.

He did not want to have a broken heart. He needed to steel his resolve. Julianne was Bennie's sister and merely that. Any other thoughts he had about her were foolish and fickle. She was *Englisch*. He was Amish. A huge divide lay between them, and no matter how much he wanted to bridge that gap, the separation would remain.

He sighed as he grabbed his mug and looked up at the sky. Clouds had covered the stars, and the night seemed as dark as his grieving heart.

EIGHTEEN

Julianne had slept little through the night. Instead, she had thought of William's crystal-blue eyes and the way he had pulled her into his arms. More than anything, she'd wanted to remain in his embrace and feel his lips on hers. If only Aunt Mary had remained inside a few minutes longer. Although Julianne would have been faced with a whole new set of problems if they had kissed, like how she would ever be able to leave Mountain Loft, and how she would survive without William.

Struggling to get the harness on Aunt Mary's mare this morning forced her thoughts back to her current situation. She hadn't hitched a horse to a buggy in three years, but Rosie was even-tempered and would hopefully overlook her clumsiness.

"You're a sweet girl, Rosie," she cooed as she patted the mare and climbed into the buggy.

"Be careful," her aunt cautioned from where she stood on the porch.

"Don't worry, Aunt Mary. Deputy O'Reilly said Mose Miller would be off the streets for quite a few days."

"You should wait until William comes in from the pasture. He'll wonder why you went to town without him."

"I've pulled him away from his work too often. Besides, I won't be gone long. I have one of *Mamm*'s baskets and will stop at Jones Grocery to buy fruit before heading to the Schwartz home. Harvey and Nancy were kind enough to gift us with the fruit basket. It's the least I can do for the deacon's wife."

"Still, I will worry about you while you're gone. Perhaps you should wait until the radiator of your car is fixed so you don't have to take the buggy."

"I'll be fine. Besides—" Julie glanced down at the blue Amish dress she had brought from her house along with the funeral garb "—no one will recognize me dressed Amish."

Her aunt laughed. "You are mistaken. Everyone will recognize your auburn hair and pretty green eyes even under your *kapp*. You were right to think of the deacon's wife and her comfort. She will be more willing to accept the basket from an Amish friend rather than someone who has left the faith."

"I was dressed *Englisch* when William and I stopped by her house so he could talk to her husband, but today I don't want her to feel unduly threatened or question whether she should accept my gift."

Aunt Mary raised an eyebrow. "Perhaps you desire to do more than dress Amish?"

"You mean return to the Amish faith?" She hesitated for a moment. "I must admit, being with you and William has brought that thought to mind."

"I see the way you look at William. Remaining *Englisch* means you have closed the door to any future you could have together."

"Yet I must be true to myself."

"*Ack*, you young people and your talk about truth. The truth is you need to accept *Gott* into your life."

"I know." Julianne reached for the reins. "But I'm not able to do that."

Her aunt sighed. "We will talk more later. Right now, I am concerned for your safety. What about the driver of the white car?"

"Mose worked for Seth Reynolds. He drives a white SUV. Deputy O'Reilly planned to apprehend him, as well. In case that hasn't happened, I'll travel along the old back road. An *Englischer* would never look for me there. Plus, I have my phone in case I need to call for help."

"I'll tell William, but I doubt that will ease his mind. Be careful, dear."

"I'll be fine."

The old road to town cut through a thickly forested area and was a pleasant ride. Julianne enjoyed the fresh air and the pretty scenery. Once in town, she tied the mare to the hitching post and hurried into the grocery.

Nancy's eyes widened, and a smile spread

across her usually glum face. "Look at you, Julianne, in your pretty Amish dress. Our Anna always longed to wear dresses like yours."

Julianne's heart warmed at the memory of her old friend. "And I was envious of Anna's fancy dresses ribbed with colorful lace."

Nancy nodded knowingly. "Your mother was concerned you might leave the faith just so you could have crinoline petticoats and taffeta dresses. Of course, she was remembering her own youth."

"I don't understand."

"We knew each other as girls." Nancy smiled as if she was recalling fond memories. "Your mother was one to push the envelope, so to speak. She wasn't sure she would remain Amish until your father asked to court her. Love made her decide to remain Amish."

"She never told me," Julianne said, surprised by Nancy's statement.

"That's the reason she wouldn't let you go with Anna and me the day we went shopping in Willkommen." Nancy's face paled. "Of course, we both know how that ended."

The day of the car crash when Anna had died. Julianne patted the woman's hand.

Tears filled Nancy's eyes. "Had you been in the car with us, I fear you would have been injured, as well."

"I didn't know you wanted me to join you."

"Of course I did, dear." Nancy acted surprised. "But your mother thought you needed to develop stronger friendships within the Amish community and suggested we not encourage you and Anna to get together again. I didn't tell Anna. It would have broken her heart."

"Mrs. Jones, I'm so sorry."

The woman pulled a handkerchief from her pocket and dabbed at her eyes. "Talking about the past upsets me. Let's focus on another subject, shall we?"

"Of course."

"Can I help you find something?"

Julianne held up the basket she was carrying. "I appreciated the fruit you and Harvey gave me and wanted to do something similar for the Widow Schwartz."

"She would like that, I'm sure." Nancy pointed to the produce area. "Gather what you need. We'll arrange the fruit and add a bow to make it extra special."

Julianne was pleased with how the basket looked when Nancy finished tying the blue ribbon.

"Tell the widow I'm thinking of her," Nancy said as Julianne left the store.

The ride to the Schwartz farm passed quickly. Basket in hand, Julianne climbed the porch and knocked on the widow's door. She knocked again when the door didn't open.

Finally, a little girl answered and stared up at Julie with big eyes and a dirty face.

"Is your mother home?" Julia asked.

The child closed the door. A few seconds later, the widow appeared. She wiped her eyes and hurried to invite Julia into the house.

"I hope you'll accept my sympathy," Julianne said, "and this basket."

The widow smiled through her tears. "How thoughtful of you. The children will love the fruit, and I will, as well."

She placed the basket on the table and glanced down at her dress, which was smudged with dust. "I have been going through Abe's papers."

"I know it's hard."

The deacon's wife sighed. "Hard and un-successful."

"You are looking for something specific?"

The widow glanced away. "I hate to admit my concern after everyone has been so thoughtful, but…"

"But what, Mrs. Schwartz?"

"Money that Abe promised would be available if anything happened to him is missing."

Julianne's neck tingled.

"I keep wondering if Abe spent it on something, but I cannot determine what that would be." She hesitated a moment and then added, "We will be fine, of course. The community will rally around us, but it is *gut* to have a bit of cash for emergencies, *yah*?"

"Yah."

Julianne was more concerned than ever on the drive home, knowing three Amish men—not including her father—had told their wives about cash for emergencies only to have the money go missing.

Dark clouds gathered overhead as her aunt's mare trotted along the old roadway. Fearing the rain would fall at any minute, Julianne hurried her along.

The clouds hid the sun, and the wind intensified. She pulled a lap blanket around her shoulders to keep warm and flicked the reins.

Julianne passed the turnoff to the Krause farm and was nearing the rear of the Miller property when she heard a car engine.

Glancing back, she saw nothing, but the sound grew louder, and her heart fluttered in warning.

Mose was in jail and a passing motorist would not cause her upset. She was being far too neurotic.

Plus, she was convinced a number of people in town still believed Bennie was a killer. Their close-minded attitudes cut her to the core. Nothing would change in Mountain Loft. The town would always think the worst about her brother.

With a heavy sigh, she glanced back again.

The vehicle came into view.

Her pulse raced. A white car with tinted windows.

She flipped the reins and pulled the mare to the side of the road, so the car could go around her. Not a car, but an SUV. The vehicle passed the buggy and pulled to a stop. Her heart pounded.

The driver remained in the vehicle for a long moment. Julianne wondered if she should turn the buggy around and race back to town. Just as she was ready to flick the reins, the driver's door opened and a man stepped to the road.

He was dressed in black and wore a red bandana.

"No," she inwardly moaned.

She could never turn the buggy in time, nor could she outrun the SUV. Instead, she leaped to the ground and ran into the woods.

He followed after her.

The brambles tugged at her dress, and branches brushed against her arms and scratched her skin. Footsteps crashed through the underbrush behind her. He was close. Too close.

She pulled in a lungful of air and pushed on. Raising her arms, she shoved aside the higher branches and ran deeper and deeper into the woods. The tree canopy overhead blocked the light, and the forest grew dark.

A clap of thunder crashed overhead, but she kept running. Lightning cracked, and rain filtered through the trees. She slipped on the wet leaves and pine straw, caught herself and hurried on.

He still chased after her.

Her side ached, and her legs were tight. She tripped and fell, and let out an *oomph*. Staggering to her feet, she kept moving.

The rain intensified. If only the man would turn back, but she could hear him stumbling through the thick underbrush. He would never give up.

The sound of rushing water came from

ahead. The fishing pond. She'd gone there often with Bennie as a child. A creek fed the pond along with the rain and run-off water. She and Bennie used to swim in the pond on hot summer days.

The cold wind billowed through the trees. Today was anything but sunny and warm, but her legs ached and she couldn't outrun the attacker.

Nearing the pond, she knew her only hope was the water.

Holding on to an overhanging branch, she stepped off the bank into the pond and forced herself into the water.

The man was approaching. He would be at the edge of the pond in seconds.

She pulled in a deep breath and ducked below the surface.

The cold hit her like a sledgehammer. She grabbed on to a root of a tree that grew along the shore and gripped it with both hands to remain submerged.

How long could she hold her breath? And when she did surface, would the man in the bandana be waiting for her?

In the murky frigid water, she thought back to her family, her mother's sweet face, her father's loving gaze, and Bennie, her dear brother, as they ran through the woods on her father's farm. Her heart swelled with love for her family.

Then another face appeared.

William.

If only he could find her before she died of hypothermia or at the hands of the man in the red bandana.

William had raced to the Schwartz farm, frustrated that Julianne would go there on her own. The widow and her children were on the porch eating apples.

"I'm looking for Julianne Graber," he had called from his buggy.

"She left some time ago."

"Was she heading home?"

"*Yah*, along the back road. Julianne said it would be a peaceful ride."

Peaceful? Except he feared someone had chased after her. Someone who had come after her time and time again.

With her car in the shop, Julianne was driving her aunt's buggy and wearing Amish clothing. Why hadn't she asked him to go with her?

He flicked the reins and encouraged Sugar to increase her speed. The old road was bumpy and rarely traveled, but he had to find Julia.

Nearing the Miller farm, he spied Aunt Mary's buggy and her mare at the side of the road. Heart in his throat, he leaped to the ground and followed the trail of broken branches. "Julianne!"

The rain had eased, but the floor of the forest was wet and slippery. He ran as fast as he could, pushing his way through the thick vegetation.

His gut tightened as he spied a piece of blue fabric caught on a limb of a tree. Julianne had been running—running for her life. If only he could find her.

"Julianne!"

Had the man grabbed her? Worse yet, had he done her harm?

Stopping in the middle of the forest, he

called her name again. The sound was like a keening death knoll that broke his heart when he heard nothing in reply.

Again, he called for her. Then again.

A lump filled his throat. He would keep searching until he found her. "Julianne."

A sound. The cry of an animal? A coyote, perhaps?

The old fishing pond was nearby. He pushed on, alert for any other sound.

"Julie, where are you?"

He ran to the edge of the water. His heart nearly stopped when he saw her. She was lying on the shore, soaking wet, shivering, her hair hanging in strands around a face that was pale as death.

Kneeling beside her, he touched her cheek. Ice-cold. He wrapped his coat around her, lifted her frigid body into his arms and ran back through the brush, praying he could get to the buggy and the blankets he kept there in time.

"Stay with me, Julie. Don't give up. Stay awake just a little longer."

At the buggy, he wrapped her in blankets,

lifted her onto the front seat and climbed in next to her. "Let's go, Sugar." He flicked the reins, then pulled Julianne into his arms again. "Back to town, Sugar. Now."

Julie trembled almost uncontrollably, and he could hear her raspy breath.

The ride to the clinic took longer than he would have liked. He stopped at the front entrance, climbed from the buggy and carried her inside. "She's been submerged in the pond."

Nurses swarmed to help. They laid Julianne on a stretcher and wheeled her into a treatment room. Dr. Norris raced past him and entered the room. The door closed.

William remained in the hallway. As the minutes passed, he became more anxious. Leaning against the wall, he hung his head in his hands and prayed.

"She's going to be okay." The doctor placed his hand on William's shoulder. "You got her here in time. Any longer out in the forest, and hypothermia would have set in. She's on one antibiotic, but I'm adding a second one. No telling what she swallowed in that water. I've called the sheriff. He'll be here soon, but she wants to see you now."

William eyes stung as he hurried into the room. Her face was as white as the sheet and mud streaked, but she looked beautiful.

She smiled, and his heart nearly burst.

He took her hand and leaned over her. "I didn't think you would make it."

"I didn't think I'd get away from the man in the bandana. You saved me again, William."

He rubbed his fingers over her cheek. "Don't scare me like that again."

She nodded. "I promise."

The sheriff pushed into the room. "I'll need to talk to her alone, Will."

He didn't want to leave Julie, but she squeezed his hand. "The doctor said I can go home soon."

While the sheriff talked to Julie, William paced the hallway. Deputy O'Reilly appeared with clean clothes for Julianne. "I stopped by your house and explained what happened to Julianne's aunt. She sent me back with a dry outfit."

A nurse took the clothing. "We'll get her changed after the sheriff is finished talking to her."

"Smithy said he'll deliver Julianne's car later tonight," the deputy explained to Will. "I've arranged for someone to drive your buggy and Julianne's aunt's rig to your house. I'll take you both home as soon as the doc releases her."

Take Julianne home?

Why would she stay in Mountain Loft when someone wanted to kill her? The town was too dangerous and held too many hidden secrets.

William wanted to protect her. Instead, she had almost died. Again. She deserved more than an Amish guy who couldn't keep her safe. She deserved someone who could protect her, although with the man in the bandana on the loose, how could Julianne ever be safe here in Mountain Loft?

Julianne couldn't get warm even wearing dry clothes and wrapped in blankets. William sat next to her in the back of the patrol car. His face was drawn. He hadn't smiled since he'd rescued her. Neither had she. There was nothing funny about frigid water and running for her life.

They passed the Miller farm and saw the flashing lights.

"The sheriff is arresting Mose," O'Reilly said. "I'm sorry we let him go after only twenty-four hours. Would have saved you a lot of problems, Julianne, if we would've kept him in jail."

Julianne thought about the man who had accosted her the first night. His build had seemed different from Mose's, but the sheriff said he'd confessed to breaking in.

O'Reilly glanced at her in the rearview mirror. "Evidently, Bennie told Emma about money your father kept at your house," the deputy explained. "She offhandedly mentioned it to Mose, who decided to steal the money for a down payment on your farm."

"I noticed an odor on his breath the night he broke in," Julianne recalled. "Maybe it was the moonshine he sampled when he manned the still."

Glancing again at the flashing lights on the sheriff's car, Julianne thought of Emma. Mose treated her badly, but she was his wife, and divorce wasn't an option for the Amish. The bishop would encourage her to forgive her husband's wrongdoing, although abuse was hard to forgive, even for a faithful Amish wife.

"The sheriff still thinks Seth Reynolds is involved," the deputy said. "At least we know he let Mose borrow his car. The sheriff will question him tomorrow. He's convinced Seth will confess to taking part in not only the moonshine operation, but also the attacks on you, Julianne."

William wrapped his arm around her and pulled her close. "You're still cold."

She nodded and snuggled closer. "I'll have some hot tea when we get back to your house."

With Mose arrested and Seth being brought in for questioning, she should feel relived, but she had hoped the attacks could have something to do with the deaths of Bennie and her father. Clearing her brother's name would have brought comfort, but that seemed impossible now. Mose's greed and desire to scare her off her property so he could buy her farm had nothing to do with the business scheme Bennie had uncovered.

Earlier at the clinic, she had overheard two of the aids talking about her brother being a killer. The rumors would never stop, no matter what she did. Each time she heard someone disparage Bennie, a knife stabbed her heart.

William's farm appeared in the distance. She turned her gaze to her own farmhouse sitting dark against the night, feeling a swell of melancholy for all that once was and would never be again.

Aunt Mary hurried to the car when Deputy O'Reilly braked to a stop in front of William's house. "I have been so worried."

Julianne stepped into her aunt's outstretched arms. "It's over, Aunt Mary. Mose wanted my farm and confessed to breaking in. The sheriff is convinced the man he works for, Seth Reynolds, is responsible for the other attacks."

"You have been through so much, Julianne. Let's go inside. I'll fix a hot cup of tea. I kept dinner warm."

"I don't want anything to eat, but tea would be good."

She waved to the deputy through the open driver's window. "Thanks for the ride, Terry."

"No problem, Julianne. Again, I regret Mose was released earlier."

"It's over."

William shook hands with the deputy and followed her inside. Aunt Mary made tea for Julianne and poured a cup of coffee for William.

"I'll take your wet clothing to the barn and wash everything later tonight."

Julianne doubted she would ever wear the Amish dress again. Still, she knew Aunt Mary wanted to be helpful, and if washing clothing brought comfort, Julianne wouldn't rob her aunt of that satisfaction.

As her aunt hurried to the barn, William reached for Julianne's hand. "I'm sorry, Jules."

"I shouldn't have gone alone to visit the Widow Schwartz, but I thought Mose was behind bars. I didn't want to disturb your work. Instead, I caused more upset."

"I'm so glad I found you."

"I'm glad, as well." She smiled weakly and squeezed his hand. "But, William…"

He raised an eyebrow. "What is it?"

"As grateful as I am for your protection and your hospitality, I cannot stay in Mountain Loft any longer."

"Mose has been arrested, Julie. The sheriff will ensure he remains in jail so he can't hurt you again."

"I know, but Mose has nothing to do with Bennie. I had hoped to clear my brother's name. That didn't happen. People will continue to talk and call him a murderer. Each time I hear a comment about him, I feel a knife stab my heart."

"What about your land?"

"Harvey said he would sell the farm for me. He even said he would buy it himself. I'll stop by the grocery on my way out of town and make certain he's still willing to help."

"So you're definitely leaving?"

She looked pleadingly at him. "Come with me, Will."

He shook his head and sighed. "This is my home, Jules."

"You can buy another home."

"My home is more than the house. It is the land my father and grandfather farmed. It is the Amish community that took me in when my *datt* was sick." He shrugged. "Because I was not yet baptized, they accepted me back and supported me during my *datt*'s decline. This is where I belong, Julianne."

"I—I thought..."

Ever since that night at the lake, she'd had deep feelings for William. Coming back and reconnecting, she'd realized those feelings had grown into something much stronger. The word *love* pulsed through her mind and surrounded her heart.

"Think about staying, Julianne. You have a house and sixty-five acres. I could help you with the farming. We could work together."

She stared into his eyes and saw the possibility of a future with William, but it meant she would need to become Amish again. How could she face the people who had known her father and her brother, people who thought Bennie was a killer, people who talked about it being *Gott*'s will that both of them died?

She pulled her hand out of Will's grasp. A lump filled her throat. She was exhausted and needed to hurry upstairs before her heart broke again. She couldn't stay in Mountain Loft. Each day would be a reminder of that terrible night. Every time someone whispered behind her back, she would know they were talking about her family. As much as she wanted to be with William, she didn't belong in Mountain Loft.

"I need sleep, William. Tell Aunt Mary I will see her in the morning."

"Please, Julianne. Stay a little longer so we can talk about this."

"There is nothing to discuss, William. You are Amish. I am not. There is no reason to make something out of that which can never be. You saved my life tonight. You did the same when you rescued me from the trash receptacle. I will always be grateful."

"It sounds as if you're saying goodbye."

Tears stung her eyes. "I am, William. There is no reason for me to stay."

"But—"

She didn't want to hear his excuses or the reasons she should remain in Mountain Loft. Without looking back, she ran upstairs and let the tears fall as she threw herself on her bed.

There was no future with William and no future without him. She would go through the motions of life, all the while knowing she had left her heart with William in Mountain Loft.

NINETEEN

The next morning, Julianne overheard William and Aunt Mary talking in the kitchen. The smell of bacon wafted upstairs, and the clatter of dishes in the sink told her they had eaten breakfast without her. Aunt Mary probably thought she needed to sleep. The truth was, Julie had remained in her room because she didn't want to see William.

Hearing the outside door slam, she hurried to the window. William walked with purposeful steps toward one of the distant pastures. Turning back for a moment, he glanced at her window. As much as she wanted to tap on the glass and wave to him, she ducked behind the curtain so he wouldn't see her. She had said goodbye last night. She couldn't endure repeating those difficult words again.

Her car sat in the drive. Smithy, true to his word, had brought it back last night. Nothing would stop her now.

Working quickly, she packed her bag and hurried downstairs. Her aunt's eyes widened when Julianne entered the kitchen carrying her bag in hand.

"Tell me you are not leaving."

"I have to leave." Julianne softened her gaze. "But I promise to visit you soon."

Aunt Mary wagged her finger. "If you do not visit me, I will hire an Amish taxi and visit you in Dahlonega."

"That would make me happy. I could show you the town and where I work. You could tour the old abandoned mines and visit the museum."

"Ack!" Aunt Mary shook her head. "We have enough gold mines in this area, *yah*? I do not need to tour that which is also in Mountain Loft."

"Maybe Ted McDonough and Brad Abbott will build a museum here in town," Julianne mused sarcastically.

Her aunt raised her brow. "A museum where you could work, perhaps?"

Julianne's heart ached. "I can't come back to Mountain Loft."

"It is because of Bennie, *yah*?"

"Yah." She smiled ruefully. "People still think my brother is a killer."

The older woman grabbed Julianne's hand. "You know this is not true."

"But that doesn't ease my pain."

"Have you told William you are leaving?"

Julianne nodded. "Last night."

Aunt Mary tilted her head. "He did not mention this at breakfast. What about your farm?"

"I'll talk to Harvey before I leave. He mentioned selling the property for me. I trust him and know he'll help me find a buyer."

Her aunt sighed. "I will pack my things, as well, but I will see you soon, *yah*?"

"For sure." Julianne handed her a card. "This is my cell phone number. The phone shack is close to your house. Call me when you get home so I know you made it safely down the mountain."

"I will call to make sure you are home safely, as well."

Her aunt lifted a strand of hair from Julianne's cheek and wrapped it behind her ear. "Your clothing from yesterday is clean. I folded your things and left them on the counter. Your car keys are there, as well."

"Thank you, dear Aunt Mary."

"You are a wonderful woman, Julianne, but you still carry the weight of grief on your shoulders. Give your pain to *Gott*. He loves you even more than I do."

Aunt Mary opened her arms, and Julianne stepped into her loving embrace. Her own mother was gone, but Julie had the love of another *gut* woman to warm her heart.

She kissed her aunt's cheek. "I need to go, but first..."

Julianne placed the laundered clothing in her bag, pulled out the envelope she and William had found in her brother's room and placed it in her aunt's hands.

"It's money Bennie saved for his future

with Emma. With Mose in jail and a baby on the way, she'll need financial help. Would you ask Will to make sure Emma gets it?"

"She'll need it for sure," Aunt Mary said as she hugged Julianne once again.

Before climbing into her car, Julie glanced at her old home in the distance. She needed to stop there one more time before she left Mountain Loft.

Turning onto the main road, she was flooded with memories, all good. She thought of the times she and Bennie had run through the pastures and played games of hide-and-seek in the wooded area behind the house. As children, they'd pretended to be spies and pirates and explorers, and had a secret knothole in an oak tree where they'd hidden tiny treasures.

She turned into her drive, parked near the back porch and stepped from her car. For a long moment, she studied the farmhouse and wished her life had taken a happier path. A happy path, instead of the painful reality of what had happened.

If only she could step back into her Amish

life before everything had changed. If she had been able to absolve her brother of wrongdoing, she and William might have had a second chance to right the wrongs of the past and embrace the future together. Now, that hope was gone.

A breeze rustled through the trees, and a shaft of sunlight fell on the old oak tree, inviting her forward. More memories assailed her as she neared the Hidden Secrets Tree, as she and Bennie had called it in their childhood.

Resting her forehead against the tree, she sighed. If only Bennie would forgive her for telling their *datt* about his meeting that night. "I'm sorry," she whispered.

Rubbing her hand over the tree's gnarly bark, she imagined Bennie's laughter and the sparkle in his eyes. The memory washed over her and brought with it a cleansing of sorts, as if some of the guilt she carried had been wiped away.

"You were a *gut* brother, Bennie."

She stood for a long moment basking in the memories, and then, pulling in a deep breath, she peered into the knothole and smiled as she retrieved a bag of toy coins Bennie claimed were gold bullion when they'd pretended to be pirates. There was also a rusty sheriff's badge for their make-believe games of cops and robbers.

Overcome with nostalgia, she clutched the items to her heart and smiled, feeling a connection with her brother. Before turning away, she checked the hole once again. Her fingers touched a hard, smooth surface. Unsure of what was hidden there, she pulled out the object.

Her heart jolted. Bennie's cell phone. The battery had long ago lost its charge, but another check of the hiding spot revealed the phone charger.

In her mind's eyes, she saw Emma pull an imaginary cell phone from her pocket and lift it to her ear.

Julianne stared at the mobile device. Her heart raced. She knew without a shadow of a doubt the evidence Bennie had collected was stored on the phone he had hidden in the old oak tree.

* * *

Julianne arrived in town and headed for Jones Grocery. Harvey wasn't there, but Nancy smiled from behind the counter. "Hello, dear, can I help you find something?"

"I'm going back to Dahlonega and wanted to talk to Harvey about my farm. He said he'd help me sell it or perhaps even buy it himself."

"Buy your farm? Oh, my." Nancy raised her hand to her throat. "I'm not sure about that."

Undoubtedly, Julianne had spoken out of turn. Not wanting to cause Nancy upset, she tried to backtrack. "Perhaps I misunderstood."

"I'll call Harvey and let him know you're here." Nancy pointed through the back hallway. "You can wait for him in his office."

"Would you mind if I charge my brother's phone while I wait?"

Nancy looked confused. "Your brother's phone?"

"I have the charger, but it didn't work in my car. All I need is an electrical outlet."

"Of course, dear. That will be fine."

Julianne remembered Harvey's office from when she was young and spent time in the grocery with Anna. The walls were covered with photos of the Joneses and their only child. The pictures of Anna tugged at Julie's heart.

She plugged in the charger and waited for Bennie's cell to engage. In a matter of minutes, the screen lit up. She touched the Home button and was prompted to enter a pass code.

What would Bennie have chosen? She tapped in his birthday, which was rejected. She tried Emma's birthday and was relieved when the phone opened. She hit the Mail icon and scrolled through a number of emails, some from William and some from Bennie's other friends in town. Before she had scrolled too far, she found a message Bennie had sent to himself.

Three files appeared when she clicked on the message. Opening the first one, her pulse quickened as she glanced at the header—Mountain Loft Investments—followed by a list of Amish names, many of which she recognized. Sums of money were typed next to each name.

Amos Koenig—ten thousand dollars.
Zachariah Beechy—twenty-five thousand dollars.
Abraham Schwartz—forty thousand dollars.

Her heart lurched. Each of the men had either gone missing or was dead. Another name farther down the list made her lean closer.

Daniel Graber—fifty thousand dollars.

She stared at her father's name. Just like the other Amish farmers, her *datt* had invested his savings, and probably the nest egg he had hidden at home, in hopes of making a profit. The bank account she had inherited after his death had revealed little return on his investments.

Getting involved in an illegal scam didn't sound like her father. He and the other Amish farmers had probably thought Mountain Loft Investments was a legitimate operation.

The door to the office opened, and Harvey stepped inside. "Nancy said you want me to sell your property?"

Before she closed the file, she glanced at the name typed on the signature line at the bottom of the investment form.

Harvey Jones.

Shocked to see him standing before her, and even more shocked to know he was the corrupt businessman, she couldn't think of anything coherent to say. She kept seeing the man who had attacked her the night she arrived home. Why hadn't she recognized Harvey?

She jammed the phone in her pocket and stumbled to her feet. "I—I need to go."

He closed the door behind him. "What's your hurry, Julianne?"

Her heart lodged in her throat. "William's waiting for me outside."

"Nancy told me you found your brother's cell phone."

She shook her head. "I don't have Bennie's phone."

"Of course you do. You could never lie." He stepped closer. "From the look on your face, you must have accessed the files he saved from my computer."

"You were looking for the hidden files that first night you attacked me, weren't you, Harvey? And again the night of the storm. Why'd you wait five years to search for the evidence?"

"Anything Bennie had taken would have gone unnoticed in an empty farmhouse as it fell into disrepair. When the county issued the new policy about abandoned property, I started to worry. Knowing you would return home made me all the more determined to find the evidence."

"Why did you do it?" she demanded, brokenhearted that the man she held in such high esteem was involved in a deadly scheme.

He shrugged. "I got into financial planning to help my Amish friends make a profit, which they did, at first. After a few bad investments, I had to work harder to catch up."

"You were using their money."

"I was trying to make up for my losses."

"Your losses of *their* money. You wanted Bennie to work with you, but he realized your investments were a way to keep you solvent. You met with him that night, didn't you?"

She saw it all play out just as she had imagined. "You argued, and when my *datt* came downstairs to investigate what was going on, you shot him."

"I didn't have a choice."

He lunged for her. She screamed and struggled to pull free. He wrapped his arm around her neck and dragged her into the rear storage area. She thrashed as he opened the walk-in cooler and shoved her into the cold interior.

"Help!" she screamed, her breath frosting the air.

"The cooler's soundproof, Julianne. No one will hear you." He tied her hands together with twine, then rummaged in her purse and pulled out her car keys. "We're going for a ride."

"You'll never get away with this, Harvey."

"I didn't kill you five years ago, Julianne, which was a mistake. I won't make that same mistake again."

Unable to keep his mind on anything except Julianne, William gave up working in the pasture and returned home. He needed to talk her out of leaving Mountain Loft, although he feared nothing he said would change Julie's mind.

He had struggled through the night, trying to find a way they could be together. He wanted her to return to the faith, but Julianne had turned her back on *Gott*. Unless she came to a better place with the Lord, she would never become Amish again.

Stepping into the kitchen, he expected

to see both women. Instead, he saw only Aunt Mary. Her face was drawn and her eyes downcast.

An ominous pall settled over him. "Where's Julianne?"

"She's gone, William. She said to thank you and tell you how much she appreciated your hospitality."

His heart lurched. "Why didn't she say goodbye?"

"She told you last night she was leaving."

"*Yah*, but I thought she meant in a day or two."

He glanced through the still-open doorway to the Graber farmhouse in the distance. "What about her property?"

"Harvey Jones said he would help her with the sale and let her know about any interested buyers. She planned to talk to him before she left Mountain Loft."

If she stopped in town, she could still be there. "How long ago did she leave?"

"Two hours at the most."

His heart sank, but he couldn't stay on the

farm and do nothing. He wanted one more chance to convince her to change her mind.

"I'm going to Mountain Loft."

"She's gone, William."

"I'll follow her to Dahlonega if need be." He started for the door. "I let her slip away from me after her father's and brother's deaths. I can't make that same mistake again."

"There's no hope, William. She doesn't want to be Amish."

"She doesn't want *Gott* in her life, that's the real problem. I pray He'll give me the words to convince her of His love. Then maybe she'll be convinced of my love, as well."

He raced to the barn and hitched Sugar to the buggy. With a flick of the reins, he guided the mare onto the main road. Catching up to Julianne in her car would be impossible, but if *Gott* willed them to be together, the impossible would come to pass.

"If only it could be so," William said with conviction. "If only."

TWENTY

William's heart sank when he didn't see Julianne's car in front of Jones Grocery. He hurried inside and waited as Nancy rang up a customer and handed the lady her purchases. Once the woman left the store, William moved to the counter.

"Have you see Julianne? She planned to stop in this morning."

Nancy's eyes widened. "Julianne Graber?"

Was there any other Julianne in town? "She wanted to talk to Harvey about her farm."

The woman averted his gaze. "You'll have to ask my husband. Harvey was here earlier."

"Where can I find him?"

She shook her head. "I'm not sure."

"Nancy, it's very important that I find Julianne."

"He had a meeting with the mayor."

"Was that after he talked to Julie?"

"I... I'm not sure."

Not sure or wouldn't tell him. Nancy Jones looked unduly anxious. Was this a bad day for her, or was she hiding something from him?

The bell rang as the door opened. Eli Krause's *datt* entered the store.

"May I help you?" Nancy seemed eager for a distraction.

The Amish farmer nodded to Will and approached the counter. "I wanted to check on my investments."

Nancy tugged at the collar of her dress. "Harvey will be back later."

"He's in a meeting with the mayor," Will volunteered.

The guy scratched his head. "I just saw the mayor at Country Kitchen."

"My mistake." Nancy laughed nervously. "He was meeting with Brad Abbott."

Mr. Krause looked confused. "Brad was having coffee with the mayor."

"Then Harvey will return soon for sure."

"I'll stop back later." Krause nodded to William and left the shop.

Nancy began unpacking a carton of canned goods.

"What's going on?" Will demanded.

She ignored his question. "I'll tell Harvey you were here."

"Did Amos Koenig and Zachariah Beechy give Harvey money to invest?"

"I don't know what you're talking about." She placed the cans on a nearby shelf.

"Both men invested money with Harvey, didn't they, Nancy?"

She dropped one of the cans and turned toward him. Her eyes were wide, and her face was tight with worry. "You can't prove anything, William."

"You mean I can't prove Harvey took money from unsuspecting Amish farmers."

"He made good investments. They made money, until—"

"Until his investments went bad. Did Amos

Koenig and Zachariah Beechy confront him when they realized he'd lost their money?"

"Of course not." She tugged at her hair.

The woman was unraveling in front of him. "Nancy, I need to find Julianne. She's with Harvey. Am I right?"

She nodded.

"Take me to them, and everything will be okay. I can help Harvey with the investments. In fact, I have a large amount of cash he could invest for me. He'll be able to pay off his debts and be in the black again."

Her face brightened.

"I want to help," he repeated. "But you need to take me to Harvey."

"Are you sure?"

"I'm positive. Harvey will be relieved. You won't have to worry anymore." He glanced behind the counter. "Where are the keys to your car?"

"In my purse." She rummaged in her handbag. "We'll take my Highlander. It's locked in the garage behind the store. Harvey never wants me to drive it, but he won't mind today."

"You lock your SUV in the garage?"

"Except when Harvey takes it for a spin at night."

William's chest tightened. "What color is your car?"

"It's a white four-door."

Good ol' Harvey Jones, a man everyone liked, had driven the car that chased after Julianne the night she arrived home. The same car that had tried to push them off the mountain.

He took the keys out of Nancy's hand. "I'll drive. You can direct me."

"Did you know Harvey's family has a gold mine? He always wanted to strike it rich. Harvey says we'll find our gold someday."

Harvey would do anything to strike it rich. Even commit murder. William had to get to him in time or Julianne would be the next to die.

The road was treacherous and steep. William kept Nancy talking to calm her nerves as they drove up the mountain.

"Harvey wanted to help the Amish farmers," she explained. "He told them he could grow their savings. He was thinking of their future and the well-being of their families."

In Nancy's warped mind, her husband was an altruist instead of a thief. All William could think of was the pain Harvey had caused and what he would do to Julianne.

"We both wanted to leave Anna with a sizable inheritance." Nancy gazed out the window and rubbed her hand over the glass. "Sometimes I see her. Anna was such a pretty child."

"How far are we from the mine?"

"The next road to the right."

William made the turn Nancy indicated. The dirt road dead-ended at the mine. Julianne's car was parked near the entrance.

"I'll talk to Harvey." Will climbed from the car. "Wait here, Nancy."

Before he had taken five steps, a car door slammed. Will glanced back and realized his mistake.

Nancy held a pistol in her hand aimed at him.

"Lower the gun, Nancy," he warned.

Her face twisted into a conniving smile. "Did you think I would let you destroy the investment company my husband created?"

"I have money to invest, remember? I can help."

"Harvey wanted someone to help him with the business, but the young man he chose turned on him."

"Bennie Graber." William kept his voice low and nodded with feigned compassion. "That's why Harvey killed him."

"Bennie didn't give him a choice. If Daniel Graber had stayed upstairs, he would still be alive, too."

She motioned Will forward. "If you want to see Harvey, start walking."

William entered the mine shaft. The floor was dirt, and the walls were shored up with old rotten timber. Just ahead, the tunnel branched right.

"Harvey?" Nancy's voice echoed in the dank and musty dimness. "I've brought someone who plans to help us."

The grocer peered back at them from the bend. "I told you to stay at the store, Nancy."

William kept moving, his gaze searching for Julianne. "I have money to invest, Harvey."

At the turn, the grocer, his shirt soiled and sweat stained, grabbed Will's arm and shoved him forward. A Coleman lantern sat on a niche in the rock.

"William!"

Hearing Julianne's voice, he glanced down. She sat propped against a rock with her hands and legs bound.

He dropped to her side. "Are you all right?"

"He's got a gun," she whispered.

Harvey wiped his brow and pulled a weapon from his waistband—a Smith & Wesson similar to the gun Ike had found clutched in Bennie's hand. "You arrived just in time to help."

He tossed Will a shovel and pointed to a hole he had dug in the dirt. "Expand the grave to hold two bodies."

Will's heart lurched. Harvey planned to kill Julianne and bury her in the gold mine. Glancing into a small offshoot tunnel, he spied two mounds of rock and rubble.

"You killed Amos Koenig and Zachariah Beechy and buried them here," he said on a hunch.

Harvey smiled. "You're a smart man. Amos and Zachariah were stupid. I tell my clients not to discuss their investments with anyone except me, but they didn't follow the rules. Amos demanded his money. Zach made the same demands some months later. Just this week, Abe Schwartz followed suit. None of them understood long-term investments."

Will needed Harvey to let down his guard. "Nancy said you need an assistant."

The grocer scowled at his wife. "You talk too much."

"All I said was that Bennie didn't work out."

"Shut up, Nancy."

Julianne moaned at the mention of her brother's name.

"Harvey, don't be hateful in front of Anna."

He growled with frustration. "Did you take your meds today?"

Nancy tugged at her hair. "I—I forgot."

Julianne glanced at William, nodded ever

so slightly and then scooted closer to the grocer's wife. "Help me, Mama."

The older woman's eyes widened as she gazed down at Julie. "What did you say, dear?"

"It's Anna. Don't you recognize me, Mama?"

Harvey frowned. "She's tricking you, Nancy. You know Anna's dead."

"He's lying, Mama." Julie shook her head beseechingly. "Don't let Daddy hurt me."

"My darling daughter." Nancy dropped to her knees and stroked Julie's hair. "Anna's come back to us, Harvey."

"She's Julianne Graber, and she knows too much."

"You lied to me before, Harvey. You said the tires were good, but I had the blow-out on the mountain road."

"That's because you were driving too fast." Visibly frustrated, Harvey stepped toward his wife and held out his hand. "Give me the gun, Nancy."

Seizing the moment, William raised the shovel and swung it against the grocer's head. Harvey gasped and collapsed to the ground. The Smith & Wesson flew out of his hand.

Nancy screamed and aimed her pistol at Will.

"Don't, Mama," Julianne pleaded. "Don't shoot."

Nancy glanced at Julianne and then at Harvey, as if seeing him for the first time. "What—what happened?"

She dropped the pistol, then cradled her husband's head in her lap. "Harvey, can you hear me?"

William grabbed the Smith & Wesson and the pistol, then untied Julianne. "Are you hurt?"

"I'm fine now that you're here."

She pulled her brother's cell phone from her pocket. "Let's hope we can get a signal."

"Call O'Reilly. And the sheriff."

William had tied up Harvey and Nancy by the time sirens sounded, and he and Julianne met the patrol car outside.

"You'll find the grocer and his wife in the mine. You'll also find where Amos Koenig and Zachariah Beechy are buried." William quickly explained Harvey's investment scheme.

"He asked Bennie to work with him," Julianne added. "My brother must have found files on Harvey's computer. Bennie sent the files to his phone."

"You're sure about that?" the sheriff asked.

She held up her brother's cell. "It's all here, and Harvey confessed to killing my *datt* and Bennie."

"You did it," William told Julianne once the sheriff said they could leave. "You cleared your brother's name."

She nodded. "I thought it would be impossible."

William smiled. "I thought finding you would be impossible as well, but with *Gott*'s help, all things are possible."

"It's too late for me to drive to Dahlonega tonight," she admitted.

"The guest room at my house is available. I'm sure Aunt Mary will be there, too." He ushered her toward her car. "I'll drive. You've been through enough."

Aunt Mary was waiting for them. "*Gott* heard my prayers," she said when William helped Julianne from the car.

"You didn't go home?" She stepped into her aunt's outstretched arms.

"One of the deputies stopped by and told me what had happened. He said William saved you."

Will shook his head. "Julianne saved herself when she pretended to be Nancy's child."

"As I listened to Henry berate his wife while we were in the mine, I realized when I stepped into my house that night, the killer didn't say Julianne. He said Anna. For a split second, Harvey thought I was his daughter, which saved my life then. Today Nancy was so confused that I used the same ploy with her and pretended to be her daughter, which saved my life again."

Aunt Mary had a pot of stew simmering on the stove, the coffee was hot and a freshly baked pie sat on the counter. William didn't think he was hungry until he started eating. Julianne ate a small first helping, then asked for seconds.

Once the dishes were done, he and Julianne went outside onto the porch.

"As you said, William, it's over."

He pulled her close. "At last."

"You saved me."

"You were the one who saved us, Julie."

"I bluffed so Nancy would let down her guard, but if you hadn't come after me, I would have died in that abandoned mine."

"I had to find you." He rubbed his finger over her cheek. "I couldn't let you leave me again."

She pulled back ever so slightly. "Don't make this harder than it has to be."

His gut tightened. "I don't understand."

"I told you, Will. I'm *Englisch* now. You're Amish. We'll remain friends, but—"

"I want to be more than friends."

"It's impossible."

"Don't say that, Julianne."

"There's no future for us, Will. We have to face reality."

She stared at him with tearful eyes and

then ran into the house. He hesitated a moment, trying to discern what had happened before following after her. By the time he got inside, she had already climbed the stairs. The door to her bedroom slammed shut.

He collapsed into the rocker near the fire. His Bible was lying open on the table next to the chair. He glanced at the text his grandmother had underlined.

All things are possible with Gott.

TWENTY-ONE

Leaving William was like suffering another death. Julianne couldn't get him off her mind or out of her heart, no matter how hard she tried. Work had occupied her days these last three weeks since she had returned to Dahlonega. Aunt Mary had come to visit, which had been a blessing, but at night, Julie kept seeing William's face as she left Mountain Loft. Although he had tried to be stoic, the pain in his expression had broken her heart.

She poured a cup of coffee and stared out her kitchen window, wondering if she would ever heal. Some wounds were too deep and never stopped festering.

As she sipped her coffee, she studied the cluster of buildings behind her apartment, wishing instead for the expansive fields and pastures that stretched around her farm-house and William's. Ted McDonough had called and offered, once again, to buy her land. Evidently, he didn't understand the meaning of no.

Her cell rang. Placing the cup on the counter, she grabbed her phone and lifted it to her ear.

"It's Paul Taylor," the caller said, quickly identifying himself.

Her pulse raced. "Is something wrong, Sheriff?"

"Nothing's wrong, Ms. Graber. I wanted to apologize."

"I don't understand."

"I didn't, either. Things sneak up on you when you get older. I didn't want to believe there was anything sinister going on in my town or that my mind wasn't as sharp as it used to be. I should have noticed and fol-lowed up on things better. I've submitted my resignation. My sister has a place near the water in Brunswick with an apartment over the garage."

"That sounds lovely."

"Before I leave Mountain Loft, I wanted to ask your forgiveness."

"Forgiveness?"

"The investigation into the deaths of your father and brother," he offered as explanation. "It's hard enough to lose loved ones. Even harder to have your brother accused of murder."

"At least the truth came out in the end, Sheriff."

"I hope that brings you some comfort."

"It does. Quite a bit of comfort."

"Well…" He hesitated, as if waiting for her to say something else.

She'd made mistakes, more than she could count, and the biggest mistake was holding on to guilt as if it was a crutch. It had kept her from embracing life to the fullest. In addition, she had held on to her upset with the sheriff and the pain his murder-suicide ruling had caused. Was she willing to let go of that which had seemingly hardened her heart?

Pulling in a cleansing breath, she made the decision to put the past behind her. "I forgive you of any wrongdoing, Sheriff, and I ask your forgiveness for anything I may have done that hurt you."

"You're a good woman, Ms. Graber. I hope you'll return to Mountain Loft soon."

Julianne stared at the phone after the sheriff disconnected. She had asked his forgiveness, which was a start. Now she needed to ask *Gott*'s forgiveness.

She walked to a small shelf where she kept a few mementoes from her past. Her Bible was there, unopened and unread since she'd moved to Dahlonega. She touched the leather cover, then pulled the small book from the shelf and held it against her heart.

Bowing her head, she said the words that would bring healing and peace. "*Gott*, forgive me."

A week later, William noticed a U-Haul trailer in the drive of the Graber home. Realizing Julianne must have rented out the farmhouse and wanting to be welcoming, he grabbed the basket she had left behind, filled it with Aunt Mary's jams and jellies

and headed to meet his new neighbors. Seeing someone else in the Graber farmhouse
would be difficult. He had to move on, but
the idea of not being with Julianne tore at
his heart.

Will sighed deeply as he walked along
the road, thinking of all that had happened
since Julie had left Mountain Loft. Mose
Miller's case was scheduled to go to trial
within the month. Seth Reynolds had been
arrested for distilling along with his uncle,
but both men had been cleared of any in-
volvement in the attacks on Julianne. Deputy O'Reilly felt sure Harvey Jones would
be sentenced to life imprisonment, and his
wife was currently under psychiatric care.
Most surprising of all was Sheriff Paul Taylor's resignation and the mayor's announce-
ment that Terry O'Reilly would be the new
interim sheriff.

Things change, William thought as he
turned at the gate and walked toward the
back porch. His mind was flooded with
memories of Julie.

Before he could climb the steps, the door

flew open and an Amish woman stood at the threshold. She had auburn hair, green eyes and a wide smile under her starched white *kapp*.

His heart nearly stopped. "Julianne!"

"I was wrong, William. I left the faith because I was mad at *Gott*, but in reality, I was grieving for my father and brother and weighed down with guilt. Aunt Mary visited me in Dahlonega, and we had long talks late into the night. She made me see I was ashamed of what I had done. Once I realized what I told my *datt* had nothing to do with his death, I could forgive myself. Sheriff Taylor called, and only then was I able to ask the Lord's forgiveness."

"The sheriff called you?"

She nodded. "Strange as it seems, the sheriff made me realize I had pushed *Gott* away, along with my faith. I also harbored a bit of animosity toward the bishop. When I talked to him, he explained *Gott* had not willed my family to die, not my mother or my father and brother. You told me death is part of life. I understand that now. I also understand that I wasn't to blame."

"You've come back to Mountain Loft?"

"I've come back to my faith. I've come back to my home." She crossed the porch and nearly ran down the steps. "I've come back to you, William."

"Are you sure?"

"Cross my heart!"

Overcome with joy, he opened his arms and pulled her into his embrace.

"I started loving you that night at the lake, William. As I grieved for my father and brother, I thought what could have been between us had been destroyed. Coming back to Mountain Loft, I realized how deeply I've always loved you. Without you, William, my life has no meaning."

He drew her closer. "I love you, Julianne. Ever since that day with Bennie when you came outside and I saw you—truly saw you—for the first time. The night at the lake only solidified what I already knew."

"And what was it that you knew?" Her eyes twinkled.

"That I wanted to court you and ask you to be my wife."

"Oh, William, that's what I want, as well."

"Will you, Julianne...?" He hesitated.

She looked at him with eager anticipation.

"Will you be my wife?"

Slipping her arms around his neck, she drew her lips near his. "Yes, William. A hundred times yes. Nothing would make me happier than to be your wife."

"I thought it was impossible," he whispered.

"Nothing is impossible with—"

She didn't finish the statement they both believed to be true, because at that moment William lowered his lips to hers and kissed her with such intensity that she had to know without a shadow of a doubt they belonged together. The painful memories had been replaced with the expectation of a future together, of children, of life lived as man and wife, putting *Gott* first and family second as they faced their tomorrows together.

"We'll combine our farms," Julianne said breathlessly.

"Aunt Mary can move into your house when we marry. It would be *gut* to have her close."

"That would make me happy."

"You make me happy, Julianne."

"Oh, William, you've made me the happiest woman in the world."

"I'm so glad you came home to Mountain Loft!"

"I came home to you, William, and wrapped in your arms is where I want to remain for the rest of my life."

* * * * *

*If you enjoyed this story,
look for these other titles
by Debby Giusti:*

Amish Christmas Search
Dangerous Amish Inheritance
Her Forgotten Christmas Past

Dear Reader,

Five years ago, Julianne Graber left home and her Amish faith. Now she's returned to Mountain Loft to sell her father's farm, but secrets abound in the former mining town. Amish farmer William Lavy is the only one willing to uncover the truth about the double homicide that took her father's and brother's lives—and he's the only one who can keep Julianne safe when someone wants her dead.

I pray for my readers each day and would love to hear from you. Email me at debby@debbygiusti.com or visit me at www.DebbyGiusti.com and at www.facebook.com/debby.giusti.9.

As always, I thank God for bringing us together through this story.

Wishing you abundant blessings,
Debby